"You okay?" Bo asked, stopping outside the interview-room door. "You're flushed and you're breathing funny."

"Oh." She quickly tried to fix that. Talk about wearing her heart on her sleeve.

"Oh?" Bo questioned.

She didn't answer. She just stared back.

"Oh," Bo finally said, and he huffed. "Yeah. We'll deal with that later."

"How?" she blurted out. Great. Now she'd just opened a box that should be left closed.

The corner of his mouth rose and he crushed his mouth against hers for just a split-second kiss. "How the hell do you think we'll deal with it?"

No smile this time. "We'll be more amicable to each other if I'm…well…having sex with you."

"Amicable," she repeated. That wasn't the word she would use. "It would be very…" And here she tried to figure out the best way to put it. "Satisfying."

"Hell, when I get you in my bed, I won't be aiming for something satisfying or amicable. I figure if we're going to screw up our lives, then it might as well be something to remember."

DELORES FOSSEN

THE TEXAS LAWMAN'S LAST STAND

TORONTO • NEW YORK • LONDON
AMSTERDAM • PARIS • SYDNEY • HAMBURG
STOCKHOLM • ATHENS • TOKYO • MILAN • MADRID
PRAGUE • WARSAW • BUDAPEST • AUCKLAND

Recycling programs
for this product may
not exist in your area.

ISBN-13: 978-0-373-74573-9

THE TEXAS LAWMAN'S LAST STAND

Copyright © 2011 by Delores Fossen

www.eHarlequin.com

Printed in U.S.A.

ABOUT THE AUTHOR

Imagine a family tree that includes Texas cowboys, Choctaw and Cherokee Indians, a Louisiana pirate and a Scottish rebel who battled side by side with William Wallace. With ancestors like that, it's easy to understand why Texas author and former air force captain Delores Fossen feels as if she were genetically predisposed to writing romances. Along the way to fulfilling her DNA destiny, Delores married an air force top gun who just happens to be of Viking descent. With all those romantic bases covered, she doesn't have to look too far for inspiration.

Books by Delores Fossen

CAST OF CHARACTERS

Lieutenant Bo Duggan—Thirteen months ago his wife was one of the maternity hostages who died, leaving him to raise their newborn twins. But Bo's world is turned upside down again when an attractive P.I. shows on his doorstep and insists one of the babies is hers.

Mattie Collier—After being outed while in Witness Protection, Mattie had no choice but to leave her newborn daughter with Bo's now late wife. Mattie knows that reclaiming her child won't be easy, but she hadn't counted on her arrival bringing out a killer or on the hot attraction between her and Bo.

Holly Duggan—Mattie's thirteen-month-old daughter. Holly doesn't even know that Mattie is her mother. The only parent she knows is her daddy, Bo.

Jacob Duggan—Bo's thirteen-month-old son gives Mattie a warm welcome, but he's too young to know that with Mattie around, he could be in danger.

Kendall Collier—Mattie's uncle, whose shady business dealings might have come back to haunt them all. Does someone from Mattie's and Kendall's past want her dead?

Marshal Larry Tolivar—He claims he wants to protect Mattie and place her back in Witness Protection, but bad things seem to happen when the marshal is around.

Terrance Arturo—A P.I. who seems to be following Mattie. But why? And who hired him?

Ian Kaplan—He works for Kendall and doesn't hide that he's in love with Mattie, but she's not sure Ian has her best interests at heart.

Cicely Carr—Kendall's wealthy fiancée, who seems willing to do anything to protect the man she loves.

Prologue

San Antonio Maternity Hospital

The gunshots stopped.

With her heart in her throat, Mattie Collier waited for more rounds of fire. They didn't come, thank God. And judging from the scene unfolding on the live news report on TV, this was the end of the hostage standoff.

The nightmare was over.

Well, one nightmare anyway.

Blinking back tears, Mattie knew it was time for her to die, *again*.

Another faked death, another run for her life. She'd done it before when she'd gone into the Federal Witness Protection Program six months earlier.

This time, it would be much, much harder.

Harder, because of her newborn baby. Her precious daughter was a mere two hours old. She was too young to be in the path of danger, and Mattie knew it was too big a risk to try to escape with her. If she failed, if they caught her, the unthinkable could happen.

On the muted TV in the nurses' lounge, Mattie could now see the police and firemen outside the four-story hospital. Reporters, too. They had their cameras aimed at the building where Mattie and the others were still hiding and waiting for the official end of the nine-hour hostage standoff.

Their captors, the gunmen who'd terrorized them for those nine hours, had stayed concealed behind ski masks, and Mattie had only gotten a glimpse of them before she and another patient had escaped and hidden in the nurses' lounge at the end of the maternity ward hall. Now, without explanation, their captors had apparently given up and perhaps even managed to get out of the building despite every attempt to stop them.

Any minute, San Antonio PD would storm the hospital to look for injured patients or perhaps even another gunman. The officers would eventually make it to the fourth floor, where she was, and if Mattie allowed them to rescue her, the photographers who were no doubt waiting outside could snap her picture. The wrong people could learn that she wasn't dead after all.

And that was a sure way to get her and her precious daughter hurt, or worse.

With her baby cradled in the crook of her arm, Mattie got to her feet. Not easily. She was still dizzy and weak from the long labor and the stress of not knowing if the gunmen were going to kill them all. The adrenaline had come and gone, leaving her with the bone-weary fatigue and sickening dread that came with an equally sickening reality. She'd barely had enough strength to change into the green scrubs that she had found in a nurse's locker, and she wasn't expecting to regain her strength anytime soon.

A fire alarm sounded and was quickly followed by water falling from the overhead sprinklers.

She glanced up at the ceiling. There were no sprinklers here in the lounge, and that gave her a jolt of panic. She cracked open the door, barely a fraction, and looked out. There were no signs of fire, just the faint smell of smoke. Thankfully, her fellow patient and she were far enough away from that smoke, and the sprinklers would hopefully smother any flames before the firemen could come in and do their thing.

Mattie took some steps, staggering. Neither the pain nor the dizziness would stop her. She knew what had to happen. And it would be the hardest thing she would ever have to do.

Mattie made her way to the leather sofa where Nadine Duggan was asleep. Mattie hadn't known the petite blonde before they'd been taken hostage while in the throes of labor. With no one to help them, Mattie and Nadine had sneaked away from the others and hidden in the nurses' lounge. Nadine and she had cried, hoped and prayed through their labors while trying to stay quiet so their captors wouldn't find them. They'd helped each other and then both had given birth there in the lounge. First, Mattie. Then, a half hour later, Nadine.

Now, Nadine had her own newborn son snuggled against her, where he'd fallen asleep after nursing.

"It's over," Mattie told Nadine, tipping her head toward the TV. "The gunmen seem to be gone, and the police are in the building."

Nadine's eyes were glazed from fatigue. "Is Bo here?"

From their whispered labor conversations, Mattie knew that Bo was Nadine's husband. Or rather "the best husband in the world," as Nadine had claimed. The love of her life. The answer to her prayers.

Mattie hoped Bo would soon be the answer to her own prayers, as well.

From what Mattie had gathered from the TV coverage, Lieutenant Bo Duggan, a cop in the San Antonio PD, had been on the way to the hospital when the ski-mask-wearing gunmen had stormed the labor and delivery ward. Nadine had been trapped inside, and Bo had been unable to get to her.

Now with the gunmen gone, Bo was no doubt tearing his way through the hostage negotiators, firemen, SWAT and reporters to get to Nadine and their child. Mattie had seen Bo on TV, and though she hadn't been able to hear his exact words, she knew he was pleading for the gunmen to release Nadine and the others. Maybe he'd been successful. After all, something had caused the gunmen to give up the hostages.

"Bo's coming," Mattie promised Nadine.

So were Mattie's tears. She couldn't stop them as she eased her baby daughter into the crook of Nadine's left arm.

Nadine's watery blue eyes widened, and she shook her head, obviously not understanding.

"Protect her," Mattie said. "Tell everyone here at the hospital and the newspapers that you gave birth to twins. Only your husband can know the truth for now."

Another shake of her head. "Wh-why?" Nadine asked.

"Because it's the only way I can keep her safe. *Please*. I have to leave. I have to try to get out before anyone sees me, but I'll be back to get her. When I'm sure it's safe, I'll be back."

Nadine ran her tongue over her chapped bottom lip and took a deep breath. "Are you in some kind of trouble?"

"I will be if anyone figures out who I am."

"Bo can help you," Nadine insisted.

"I don't doubt that he'd try. But all it would take is one picture of me. Or for someone out in that crowd to recognize my face. That might even include the police. The world is watching, Nadine, and I can't risk being seen." And Mattie knew for certain that she couldn't trust her point of contact, a federal marshal, in the Witness Protection Program.

Not after what had happened.

Mattie swallowed hard. "Will you protect my baby?"

Nadine closed her eyes and nodded. Mattie heard the racing footsteps in the corridor. There were frantic shouts. One of them came from a man calling out for Nadine. Bo, no doubt.

Mattie's time was up.

She took one last look at her baby and leaned down and kissed her warm, rosy cheek. And with her heart in shreds, she did the only thing she could do to make sure her child would survive.

Mattie turned and left.

Chapter One

Thirteen Months Later

Lieutenant Bo Duggan didn't like what he saw in the rearview mirror of his SUV. A black van had been several vehicles behind him since he pulled out of the parking lot of San Antonio Police headquarters ten minutes earlier. The van was still there.

Maybe it was a coincidence.

Maybe not.

Bo didn't slow down or speed up. He simply continued his fifty-five-mile-per-hour pace on the drive home. Except he wouldn't go home just yet. Not with the possibility of that van on his tail.

As a veteran SAPD cop and head of the Special Victims Unit, it was always a possibility that someone was dissatisfied with the outcome of a case and wanted to bring that personal grudge to Bo's doorstep. But he wouldn't let it get that far. He already had enough to manage with the other crazy things happening in his life.

What the hell was going on anyway?

The day before, he'd learned someone was running a cyber-investigation on him. A *deep* one. From an unsecured computer at a coffeehouse, no less. He was still trying to get a list of possible suspects from the partial fingerprints taken from that keyboard. Then someone had tried to break into his SUV while it was in the parking lot at police headquarters.

Now this.

Slipping his phone from his pocket, Bo called one of his sergeants to inform him of the situation and to give him the van's license plate number to run through the database. Bo's second call was to his house, and as he expected, the nanny, Rosalie, answered.

"Rosalie, I don't want to scare you, but are all the doors and windows locked, and is the security system turned on?" Bo asked.

"Yes." But he could tell from her hesitation that she was already alarmed. Probably because he hadn't been able to keep the concern out of his voice. Still, better to be safe than sorry. "Why?"

"Just a precaution." He checked to make

sure the black van was still there. It was. "Keep everything locked up tight, and don't let anyone in unless you hear differently from me."

There was more hesitation. "I'm sorry, but someone's already here."

His stomach knotted, and he pushed his foot to the accelerator. "Who?"

"Madeline Cooper, the woman who's interested in buying the house across the street. Remember, she called yesterday to make an appointment with you so she could ask some questions about the neighborhood? I let her in about five minutes ago."

Bo didn't relax. He was expecting Ms. Cooper, just not this soon. And not with that van following him.

"Tell our visitor I'll get there as soon as I can," Bo explained to Rosalie. "And if anyone else calls or comes by, get in touch with me immediately."

"You're scaring me, Bo. What's going on?"

"I'll explain it all when I get there. Right now, I just want to take a few precautions and make sure you and the kids are safe."

He clicked End Call and was about to call for backup before he stopped the van and confronted whomever was inside, but he realized that wouldn't be necessary. The van made a right turn, off the main highway, and disappeared down a side street.

Bo blew out a long breath and wanted to dismiss the incident as mild paranoia on his part, but something in his gut told him he had reason for concern. After twelve years of being a cop, the one thing he'd learned was to trust his gut.

He pressed a little harder on the accelerator while he kept watch around him, to make sure that van didn't resurface. It didn't. Bo made the turn into his neighborhood without any sign of it or any other suspicious vehicle. However, in front of his ranch-style house there was an unfamiliar two-door blue Ford.

Ms. Cooper's probably.

He would quickly answer his prospective neighbor's questions and send her on her way.

Rosalie met him at the door that led from the garage and into the laundry room. Oh, yes. She was concerned. Normally, Rosalie was cool and calm under pressure. But Bo saw the stress, and the tenseness only accented the wrinkles at the corners of her eyes.

"Everything okay?" Rosalie asked.

"Yeah. How are the kids?"

"Fine. They're playing in the nursery." She glanced down at the monitor she held in her hand. She carried it with her whenever she wasn't with the twins so she would be able to hear them no matter where she was in the house. "So, why did I have to make sure the doors and windows were locked?"

"I thought this black van was following me. I was wrong." Bo kept it at that, but Rosalie's raised eyebrows let him know that she would want to discuss this further. "Where's our guest?"

"Living room."

Bo headed in that direction, and he kept his jacket on so that it would shield his shoulder holster and gun. Best not to alarm Ms. Cooper in case she was squeamish about such things.

He found her just where Rosalie said she would be. Not seated, but standing by the limestone fireplace, where she was looking at a framed photo. He'd forgotten the photo was there, but then he rarely went into this room. Heck, for that matter, he rarely had guests. Between fatherhood and his job, there wasn't much time for anything else.

Madeline Cooper turned. Their eyes met, and Bo made a split-second cop's assessment of her. Tall, about five-nine. Average build.

Shoulder-length, straight brown hair. Green eyes. A full mouth. Very little makeup, just a touch of pink color on her lips. She wore matching olive-green pants and a sweater. The outfit was nondescript. Definitely not flashy.

She was not a woman who wanted to draw attention to herself.

But something about her caught Bo's attention.

"Do I know you?" he immediately asked.

"No." Her answer was immediate, as well. Maybe too immediate.

"You look…" Bo didn't know where to go with that. Several things came to mind, including, much to his surprise, that she looked damn attractive. But what also came to mind was that she was "…familiar."

"Oh." It was her only response.

Bo was ready to launch into more questions, but his phone rang. He pulled it from his jacket pocket and looked at the screen. It was Sergeant Garrett O'Malley from headquarters.

"Please excuse me a second. I need to take this call. Duggan," he answered after his guest nodded.

"I ran the license plate on that black van you thought might be following you," O'Malley informed him. "It must be fake. No record of it."

Hell. That was not what Bo wanted to hear. "What about the van itself—was it stolen?"

"That's my guess. I checked, and there were two black vans reported stolen in the last twenty-four hours."

Bo didn't like that, either. "Keep digging. Try to locate that vehicle. And call me if you find out anything else." He kept his instructions vague since he had an audience nearby. Madeline Cooper seemed to be hanging on his every word.

"Is there a problem?" she asked, her forehead bunched up.

"No problem." At best, that was a hopeful remark. At worst, a lie.

He might not know which was the truth for a while.

Bo walked closer, studying her and trying to figure out why bells the size of Texas were going off in his head.

"You have a lovely home," she commented. She folded her arms over her chest and tipped her head to the photo on the mantel. "That's your wife?"

Bo glanced at the photo of Nadine. She sported a grin from ear to ear, because that picture had been taken the day she learned she was pregnant.

"My late wife," he corrected. "She died not long after giving birth."

"I'm so sorry for your loss." It sounded heartfelt, as if the loss had been hers, as well. Strange. "Do you have a son or daughter?"

"Both. I have twins."

She glanced away but not before Bo saw something flicker through her eyes. What, exactly, he didn't know, but it didn't seem to be a normal reaction.

"I remember your name now," she continued. "Wasn't your wife at the San Antonio Maternity Hospital during that hostage standoff?"

Bo let the question dangle between them for several seconds. It was definitely an uncomfortable silence, and if he'd had any doubts that his guest was nervous, he didn't have them after that. "That's right. My wife had the babies by herself while hiding in a nurses' lounge. She had internal bleeding and died."

The lack of emotion in his tone certainly didn't mean there was a lack of emotion in his heart. No. Losing Nadine had been the most difficult thing he had ever faced. If it hadn't been for the babies, he would have shut down and died emotionally right along with her. But he'd survived for their children and because that's what Nadine would have expected him to do.

"So, you had questions about the neighborhood?" Bo asked, changing the subject.

She nodded. "Um, is it safe?"

He thought of the van and hesitated. "I'm a cop. I wouldn't be living here with my children if it wasn't."

Another nod. She moistened her lips. Hell. That mouth was so familiar. Where had he seen it before?

"Are you from San Antonio?" he asked.

"No. Born and raised in Dallas, but for the past two years I've been traveling so much that I don't really have a place to call home."

"No family?"

There it was. Another flicker in her eyes before she glanced away again. "No family."

"You're not a very good liar." Bo hadn't intended to be so blunt, but frankly he was tired of this conversation. For a woman who wanted to know about the neighborhood, she didn't have much interest in it. "Now, why don't you tell me why you're really here?"

She opened her mouth. Closed it. Stared at him. And looked even more uncomfortable.

He knew how she felt. Bo was uncomfortable, too.

He stared at her, waiting for an explanation that one way or another he was going to get. He wouldn't let her leave until he knew if she were connected to that van. He was about to toss that particular accusation at her, when something flashed in his head.

And he knew where he'd seen that face and that mouth.

"I know why you look so familiar," he told her. "The surveillance video at the hospital."

She shook her head. "What video?"

"The one I studied a thousand times after the hostage standoff. A woman wearing green scrubs left the area of the nurses' lounge only seconds before I got there. The hair is different, darker, but the mouth—it's the same."

She didn't deny it. In fact, her body language confirmed it. "I have a problem," she practically whispered. "A serious one."

"Yeah, you do. You left the scene of a crime, lady, and the police want to question you. Hell, *I* want to question you. What were you doing in that nurses' lounge with my wife and newborn babies?"

She stood there, blinking hard as if fighting

back tears. "I was a hostage, too. I was trapped there like everyone else on the ward."

Bo hadn't known what answer to expect, and he wasn't sure yet if he believed her. After all, she'd fled the scene, and people didn't usually do that sort of thing unless they were running from the law. But there was something in her voice. Something in her eyes. Some deep pain. Bo understood that and knew she probably wasn't faking it. He'd already determined she wasn't much of a liar.

He went closer to her so he could keep watch with his lie-detector eyes. "You were with my wife?"

"Yes." She sank down onto the sofa and looked at her hands. "After the gunmen stormed into the hospital ward, they fired some shots at the ceiling. People ran. Obviously, there was chaos. And Nadine was in the labor room next to me. Our labors were just starting so we were able to get out of our beds and hide."

Each bit of information was a mixed blessing. For months, he'd wanted to know what Nadine had endured in those last hours, but since she'd never been able to tell him herself, he had been the one to try to fill in the blanks. As a cop, those blanks had been filled with gruesome images. Now, he had the chance to learn the truth. Well, maybe.

If this woman was telling the truth.

Because his legs suddenly felt unsteady, Bo had to sit, as well. He took the chair across from her. "How did you get from the labor rooms to the nurses' lounge?"

"The gunmen were trying to gather everyone into the hall outside the delivery suites. Nadine and I waited until the gunmen were in one of the other rooms, and that's when we left. We used the back hall and followed it to the nurses' lounge."

She fidgeted with the clasp on her purse, finally got it open, extracted a mint and popped it into her mouth. "There was a TV in the lounge, and we were able to figure out what was going on."

Yes. He remembered the TV. It was still on with the volume muted when he got to Nadine. "You didn't try to contact anyone?"

"There was no phone in the lounge, and neither of us had our cells with us. We'd left them in the labor rooms. Then, it wasn't long before the pain made it impossible to try to escape. So, we stayed put...and helped each other."

Just hearing this reopened all the old wounds. The pain. Hell. Several hours before the hostage standoff had begun, Nadine had called him from her routine doctor appointment. Her cervix was dilated, she'd said, and the doctor wanted to go ahead and admit her to the hospital.

Bo knew he should have been there to protect her. And he would have been if there hadn't been a damn traffic accident. That fifteen-minute delay had meant the difference between life and death. Because if he'd been there at the hospital, he could have gotten Nadine the help she needed, and she might not have died from complications.

He pushed aside those regrets and focused on his guest. "Why are you really here? And please don't try to lie and say it's because you're interested in the neighborhood."

She nodded, paused again. "I wanted to talk to you about what happened in the nurses' lounge."

"Good. Because I'm all ears. And while you're at it, why don't you explain why you fled the scene?"

Silence. But that didn't mean she didn't have a response. There was plenty of nonverbal stuff going on. Increased respiratory rate. Her pulse, working on her throat. Bo didn't care for any of it. Nor did he care for her. This woman clearly had some secrets, and he didn't plan for them to be secrets much longer.

He came out of the chair, startling his guest with his abrupt movement. Ms. Cooper jumped to her feet and looked ready to run, but Bo caught on to her shoulders to stop her.

"You will tell me what happened," he insisted. But then he got a sickening thought. "Did you know the gunmen? Were you their partner?"

Her eyes widened. "No."

"And why should I believe you?"

She didn't get a chance to answer. That's because they heard the rushed footsteps.

Both looked in the direction of the sound, and a moment later Rosalie appeared in the entryway of the living room. "Hate to disturb you, but it's important." There was already alarm on her face, but it went up a notch when the nanny noticed their positions. Bo still had her by the shoulders.

"What's going on here?" Rosalie asked.

He turned his attention back to Ms. Cooper. "I'm not sure."

"Well, whatever it is, I hope it can wait," Rosalie insisted. From the other end of the hall, Bo could hear his son, Jacob, babbling and playing. "You said something about a black van when you came in. You thought it might have been following you?"

That grabbed his attention. Bo let go of the woman's shoulders and turned toward Rosalie. "Yes. Why?"

Rosalie aimed her trembling hand in the direction of the front door. "Because a black van just pulled up in front of the house."

Chapter Two

Mattie's heart dropped to her knees.

No, no, no! This couldn't be happening. They couldn't have found her this fast.

Bo reacted like a cop. He whipped his gun from the shoulder holster that was concealed beneath his jacket.

"Go to the babies," he told the nanny. "Call Garrett O'Malley at headquarters. I want a unit out here now." Then he headed for the front door.

Mattie followed him. She eased her snub-nose .38 from her purse and braced herself for the worst. However, she hadn't counted on the worst coming from Bo himself.

He turned around, lightning fast, and with his left hand caught on to her right wrist. Before she even knew what was happening, he tore the gun from her hand.

"What the hell are you doing with this?"

he snarled getting right in her face. So close that his body brushed against hers.

Mattie pretended not to notice the contact. "I have my reasons for carrying a gun. And you might need backup if there's danger."

"I don't want or need backup from you. Get in the living room and stay there."

Mattie didn't try to wrestle her gun away from him, not that she would have succeeded anyway. He outsized her by at least seven inches and seventy-five pounds. But despite being outsized, she disobeyed his order.

She went to the front door and looked out one of the beveled glass sidelight windows. Even through the distortion of the bevels and the dusky light outside, she had no trouble seeing that black van. What she couldn't see was who was inside it. The heavily tinted windows prevented that.

"What do you know about this?" Bo asked, joining her. Well, actually he muscled her out of the way and looked out for himself.

"Nothing…specifically. Maybe nothing at all."

That earned her a glare from his narrowed brown eyes. "Then you'd better get into *un*specifics, even if they involve nothing at all."

Mattie tried to keep her chin high, though

it wasn't easy. "Later. After we take care of this."

Whatever *this* was.

It could be someone from Witness Protection, or her family, or maybe the men who'd been hunting her. None of these was a good option. Unfortunately, with her luck she didn't think it would be a van of Girl Scouts selling cookies.

From the end of the hall, Mattie could hear the sounds of children playing. Happy sounds. The nanny obviously hadn't frightened the children with her alarming news about the van. That was good. Now Mattie had to make sure it stayed that way. She didn't want the children upset or anywhere near the possible danger.

Despite Bo's grunt of obvious disapproval, Mattie stayed by the sidelight window. "How long before the police unit arrives?" she asked.

"Soon." He slipped her .38 into his jacket pocket. "Once they're here, I'll go out and have a chat with whoever's in that van. And then, Ms. Cooper, I'm taking you to headquarters for an interview and possibly even an arrest for carrying a concealed weapon."

Mattie couldn't go to headquarters, of course. She couldn't risk being seen. If she couldn't convince Bo otherwise, then she'd have to figure a way out of there. But she didn't want to leave. Not with so much unfinished business.

Or with so much at stake.

Bo volleyed glances between the van and her. He had a unique way of making her feel like a criminal.

Unfortunately, that wasn't all.

He also had a unique way of making her feel like a woman.

It probably had something to do with all that testosterone emanating from him. Yes, he was a man. As alpha as they came. Tall, dark brown hair. Oh, and dangerous, too. Not the kind and gentle soul that Nadine had described. But Mattie saw the appeal.

Or rather, she *felt* the appeal.

And she gave herself a good mental tongue-lashing for it. There was no room in her life for Bo Duggan or any other man.

After she had another look to make sure no one was coming out of that van, Mattie stepped back, putting some distance between her and the hot, glaring cop.

And then she saw it.

The photo on the wall.

She probably hadn't noticed it when she first came in because Rosalie had quickly ushered her to the living room. But Mattie saw it now. It was a picture of two babies.

A boy and a girl.

Both were around a year old. Both smiling for the camera. The boy had dark brown hair and was a genetic copy of Bo Duggan, right down to his already intense eyes.

And then there was the little girl.

Brown hair, as well, but hers was shades lighter than the boy's. Green eyes, not so much intense but filled with curiosity. She was so beautiful.

So precious.

Mattie heard the sound escape from her throat. Part moan, part gasp. A paradox of emotions flooded through her. The unconditional love mixed with the heart-wrenching pain of how much time she'd already lost.

She felt the movement next to her. It was Bo, although she had to blink back the tears just to see his face.

He was scowling.

And worse, he was puzzled and almost certainly on the verge of demanding answers. Mattie wasn't ready to give him those answers just yet. First, she had to lay the groundwork. She had to convince him—somehow—to help her.

"The van," she reminded him, looking back

out the window. It was still there. No open doors.

Bo returned his attention to the menacing vehicle, as well, and the silence sliced right through the foyer. "Who's out there?" he asked.

She had to clear away the lump in her throat before she could speak. "I honestly don't know."

"But it's related to you?"

"Maybe. But I don't think so. I've covered my tracks well. Plus, as you said, the van followed you. There shouldn't be a connection between me and you."

Mattie prayed that that was true. It didn't mean it was. Someone could have put one and one together and that would have led them to Bo. And to that precious little girl in the picture.

"Have you been followed before?" Mattie asked.

"No." He was adamant enough about it, but there was something that made her keep pushing.

"You're sure?"

He cursed under his breath. "Someone's been looking into my personal info. And yesterday someone tried to break into my SUV."

"Yesterday," she repeated. Mattie didn't like the timing. Yesterday was when she'd called Bo's house and asked for an appointment to see him.

She caught some movement on the street and spotted the white police cruiser. It came to a stop behind the van.

"Wait here," Bo ordered. But he didn't just order it. This time he snared her gaze, and there was trouble in his eyes. Trouble that dared her to defy him.

Mattie stayed put. Besides, it was possible that whoever was in that van would want to shoot her on sight. She didn't want to die, and she didn't want bullets coming anywhere near the children.

Much to her surprise, the driver of the van didn't slam on the accelerator and speed away. She watched as the person inside rolled down the window. Bo approached, his gun aimed and ready. The two uniformed officers who got out of the cruiser had their weapons trained on the van, as well.

When the window was completely lowered, she spotted the man inside. Scraggly salt-and-pepper hair. Long, thin face.

He was a stranger.

That didn't mean he wasn't a gun hired by someone who didn't qualify as a stranger. It wouldn't be the first time a gunman had been paid to come after her.

"Is everything okay?" she heard someone ask.

She looked over her shoulder and spotted Rosalie. The sixty-something-year-old nanny with the sugar-white hair was in the doorway of one of the rooms down the corridor. She had the little boy in her arms, his legs straddled around her thin hip.

Mattie's heart lurched, and she waited. Breath held. Hoping to see the other child. And then hoping that she didn't. Not at this moment with the van out there.

"The police are here," Mattie relayed. "Bo should be back soon."

Rosalie nodded and disappeared into the room, where she'd hopefully be safe with the children if bullets started flying.

Mattie forced her attention back on the van. The driver was smiling. His demeanor was almost apologetic. He even laughed about something one of the officers said. Bo didn't share the laugh, but he did lower his weapon, and then he said something to the uniformed officers before turning to walk toward the house.

Mattie opened the door for him but stood

to the side so that neither the officers nor the van driver could see her.

"The guy says he's interested in buying the house across the street," Bo announced. "That seems to be the lie of the day, huh?"

"You think he's lying?"

"Maybe. But even if he's not, those are fake plates on his vehicle. He'll need to explain that to the officers." He re-holstered his gun. "And speaking of explaining, let me check on Rosalie, and then I can call someone to stay with her while I take you down to headquarters."

"No." She grabbed his arm to stop him from heading to the nursery. "If you take me there, you'll be signing my death warrant."

He couldn't have possibly managed a more skeptical look. "I'm a cop, not a killer."

"There are others, though, who would love to pull the trigger." Mattie wished she'd rehearsed this or at least figured out the best way to approach what she had to say. Of course, maybe there was no best way.

He shook off her grip and turned, practically trapping her against the wall. "Did you have something to do with the men who took the hostages at the hospital?"

"No. I told you that I was one of the hostages."

"Madeline Cooper," he said as a challenge.

"Mattie," she offered, though she knew this wasn't going to turn into a friendly visit.

"Mattie," he repeated. "Your name wasn't on the list of patients who were in the ward during the hostage standoff."

"Because I left before the police arrived."

"Yeah. I know." His eyes narrowed. "And why would you do something like that?"

Mattie answered his question with one of her own. "Can I trust you?"

"As much as I can trust you," he warned, his eyes narrowing even more.

If she'd had a choice, she would have backed off then and there. But she didn't have a choice. "I was in the Witness Protection Program."

He hesitated only a heartbeat. "I want your case number so I can verify it."

"The number doesn't mean anything anymore. There was some kind of leak, and someone found out my new identity and location. Right before the hostage situation, that someone tried to kill me. I escaped and went to the hospital. The trauma must have triggered my labor. When I checked in, I used a fake name, obviously, and I said I didn't have my insurance card with me."

"You think the ski-mask-wearing SOBs were really after you?"

She shook her head. "No. At least I don't think so." From what she'd read about the case in the past thirteen months, the gunmen had been there to break into the lab and tamper with some DNA evidence. Nothing related to her.

"I couldn't just let the cops find me there at the hospital that day," she explained. "My former boss believes I'm dead, and if they'd learned differently—"

"Who's your former boss?"

She decided to tell him the truth, because maybe this would help her cause. "Kendall Collier."

Those cop's eyes darkened. He obviously recognized the name. "You're not Madeline Cooper. You're Mattie Collier. And two years ago you testified against Kendall Collier."

"Yes." Her boss, her uncle. And also someone who'd gotten involved with an illegal arms dealer and gotten off scot-free because of a technicality. "I have reason to believe that Kendall, or someone else, will kill me if anyone learns I'm alive. That's why I left the hospital."

He made a sound deep within his chest to indicate he was thinking about what she'd said. Processing it. She could see the moment that *the* question came to him. It didn't take long.

"On the video, you didn't have a baby with you. You were alone. What happened to your child?"

Mattie considered several ways she could go about this, but those ways all led to the same inevitable end. It was an end that Bo Duggan was not going to like.

She pointed to the picture on the wall. "My daughter is here with you. You've been raising her. But I've waited long enough, and I want her back."

Chapter Three

Bo hadn't thought there could be too many more surprises today, but he was wrong. He was also obviously dealing with a liar or someone in need of medication.

But Mattie Collier seemed to be lucid.

Well, except for that part about him having her child. There wasn't a chance that was true. No lucid woman would be saying that.

"Nadine had twins," he spelled out for her. "A boy and a girl."

Mattie shook her head. "No. Nadine had a son that I helped deliver. I had a daughter. And when I realized that I had to get out of that hospital or be killed, I knew I couldn't risk taking my child with me."

"So you put your newborn baby in the arms of my unconscious wife?" Bo didn't even try to take the sarcasm and skepticism out of his voice.

"She wasn't unconscious when I left. Tired

and sleepy, yes. But conscious. We talked." Mattie huffed and pushed her hair away from her face. "Nadine agreed—she was to tell you about what I was doing. But only you. And then I told her when it was safe, I'd come for the baby."

Bo couldn't even let himself fathom that this might be true. It wasn't. Jacob and Holly were his. They were his life. And he'd already ascertained that Mattie Collier was a liar. The trouble was, he couldn't quite figure out why she'd come up with this particular lie.

Maybe to get his help with her Witness Protection problem?

Perhaps. She was obviously troubled and in trouble. But it seemed an outlandish approach to get his help.

And why did he want to help her?

She'd riled him with her accusation about being Holly's mom. She'd also riled him with her stream of lies and her connections to an alleged lowlife scumbag like Kendall Collier, someone that Bo would prefer not to have introduced into the lives of his children.

Still, Mattie had that vulnerable look about her, and he hoped like the devil that vulnerability was all there was to it. This wasn't a man-woman thing.

Was it?

But then he rethought that question. It couldn't be that. Other than a passing glance, he hadn't noticed another woman since Nadine.

"Do you have any proof whatsoever about what you're saying?" he demanded.

"No. But you can get proof by doing a DNA test on my daughter. I brought the kits with me."

"*My* daughter," he corrected. "Holly is mine. Both babies have O positive blood type—that matches mine."

"O positive is a common blood type." She stepped closer. "I know this is hard for you to accept—"

"It isn't hard, because I won't accept it. But I will ask why you're doing this. Do you think if you have some kind of emotional hold over me that I'll do whatever it takes to keep you out of the path of your uncle and his hired guns?"

Mattie stepped back as if he'd slapped her. "Even you can't keep me out of Kendall's path. An entire team of federal agents failed. I failed."

"Ahhh. So, by your own admission a dangerous situation still exists in your life. Yet, according to your delusional plan, you told

Nadine that you'd come for the baby when it was safe."

He expected to see some anger in her eyes, especially since he'd just caught her in another lie. But there was no anger. Only weariness and fatigue.

She leaned back against the wall. "I have a friend who works in the Office of Vital Statistics in Austin, and she told me that someone is searching through birth records for the time period my daughter was due to be born. That someone is looking for her as a way to get to me, and judging from the records they're searching now, they're getting close to finding her. If I stay in hiding, I can't protect her, and protecting her is my first priority. That's a promise I made to her father just hours before he was murdered."

"Your story just keeps getting better and better," he mocked. Though he wouldn't put it past a criminal like Kendall Collier to commit murder. Bo didn't personally know the man, but from what he'd heard, Kendall was capable of just about anything.

Which only weakened Mattie's story.

"If you're telling the truth," Bo explained, "you wouldn't be here. A mother wouldn't put her baby in that kind of danger."

"A mother without a choice would have," she countered. "I don't have a choice."

"I beg to differ. You can turn and walk out that door right now." Of course, he wouldn't let her do that. If she was going anywhere, it was to police headquarters for a long hard interrogation.

"I've been living in fear for a long time." Her voice was strained and low now. "I worried that right after the hostage situation, the hospital would do DNA tests on all the babies. I thought my secret would be discovered then."

"How do you know the hospital didn't do tests?" Bo snarled.

"If they had, then you'd know that the little girl in the picture is mine."

She had him there. But some of the babies had been tested, those in the newborn unit that had been evacuated because the gunmen had set a fire near it before they escaped. And the other group that had been tested was those newborns that had been physically separated from their mothers at any time during the standoff.

That hadn't been the case with Nadine.

Bo and the other officers had found her and the babies in the nurses' lounge. Alone. It was obvious Nadine had given birth, and it was equally obvious that she was holding her babies in her arms.

Mattie glanced in the direction of the nursery when one of the babies fussed, but the noise soon stopped.

"Nadine didn't say anything when you got to her?" Mattie asked.

"Not much."

"But she said something," she pressed.

Oh, yes. Nadine had said something. Something that Bo had replayed in his head a million times. Words that he would never forget.

We have to protect her.

Not *them.*

Her.

The comment had puzzled Bo, but he'd dismissed it as the ramblings of a traumatized, dying woman. Nadine had meant to say *them.* The twins. Just as she'd meant to tell Bo that she loved him. But there hadn't been time, and Nadine hadn't had the energy to speak anything else.

"What did she say?" Mattie whispered. She was begging. And there were tears in her eyes, though she quickly blinked them back.

Bo didn't like those tears. They seemed genuine. The real McCoy. Still, he wasn't ready to cut her any slack. Not with what was at stake.

"I'll tell you what Nadine said," he countered, "when you tell me why you're really here."

Mattie was apparently still contemplating that when he saw the movement out of the corner of his eye. Rosalie stepped from the nursery. And she wasn't alone. She was carrying Jacob, and Holly was peeking around Rosalie's skirt.

"Is that van gone?" Rosalie asked.

Bo nodded and went toward her. He didn't want Mattie seeing Holly. But it was too late. She obviously saw the child, because Mattie went in that direction, as well.

He blocked her from moving any closer.

"What's wrong?" Rosalie demanded.

Bo locked eyes with Mattie, but he addressed his comment to the nanny. "Just wait in the nursery."

"You keep dodging the question, Bo," Rosalie answered. "And I think it's time you told me what's going on. I have ears, you know. I can hear what this woman is saying. Well, most of it, anyway."

Bo had no idea what to say to that, and it turned out that an immediate response wasn't required. That's because Holly squealed "Da

Da" and toddled toward him. She had just taken her first steps two days before, so when she wobbled, she fell to the floor and crawled toward Bo.

Jacob followed her lead, babbled "Da Da" as well and wiggled and squirmed so that Rosalie let him down. Jacob had been walking for nearly a month now but still had some trouble mastering the carpet in his bare feet.

Holly made it to Bo first. Her loose brown curls danced around her beaming face, and despite everything else going on, Bo's bad mood melted away. He scooped up his daughter in his arms and got rewarded with a sloppy kiss on his cheek. A moment later, Jacob reached him, as well, and both of Bo's arms were suddenly filled with the children he loved more than life itself.

He looked at Mattie. This time, she wasn't successful in blinking back those tears. She reached out, her fingers going straight toward Holly's curls, but it was Rosalie who snagged her wrist.

"You said some powerful things," Rosalie acknowledged. "What I want to know is why you're saying them."

Mattie kept her attention nailed to Holly. "Because it's the truth."

Rosalie met Bo's gaze, and he didn't see the

immediate dismissal that he hoped would be there. He kissed the babies again and passed them back to the nanny. "I need to clear this up with Ms. Collier."

Rosalie looked ready to argue, but thankfully she didn't. She pulled both kids into her arms and headed back down the hall.

"I was going to name her Isabella," Mattie said before he could speak. Her voice cracked. "But Holly suits her. It's a good fit."

He didn't want to hear any of this.

"This ends now," Bo quickly told Mattie. "I've already wasted enough time. If you were really Holly's mom, you wouldn't have come here."

"I told you I didn't have a choice. I've been keeping tabs on my uncle and his cronies, and I have reason to believe that Kendall or someone else has made the connection between your wife and me."

There it was. The feeling of being punched in the gut. "And how would he have done that?"

"I'm not sure. Maybe that hospital video. Maybe by talking to eyewitnesses who were able to give him a description of me." She paused. "As I told you, someone has been researching all the babies born around the time my child was due. It's possible Kendall knows that you have my child. And if he knows that, then it won't be long before he comes after her. Because he'll probably try to use Holly to get to me."

Every muscle in his body tensed. Bo couldn't bear the thought of anyone being a threat to his child.

"I still don't believe you," he said, enunciating each word so that she wouldn't misunderstand.

"Just think this through," she countered. "Nadine and you must have known she wasn't carrying twins."

"We didn't. There were no ultrasounds. Nadine had read a lot of articles about ultrasounds, and she was worried they might not be a hundred percent safe. Something to do with the way the high-frequency waves could maybe alter cells. Even though there's no conclusive evidence that an ultrasound would be harmful, Nadine didn't want to take the risk unless it was absolutely necessary."

Mattie cleared her throat. "If what I'm saying isn't true, then why else would I have been in that maternity hospital?"

He could think of a reason. A bad one. Maybe she'd been there to assist the gunmen. But if so, then why hadn't she gone with them?

Or maybe she had.

Keeping an eye on her to make sure she didn't go after Holly, Bo took out his phone, scrolled through his numbers and tapped Sergeant Garrett O'Malley's personal cell.

"Bo, have you got ESP or something, because I was about to call you," O'Malley answered, obviously seeing Bo's name and number on his caller ID. "You're not going to like this, but the guy in the black van hasn't even gotten here, and his lawyer has already arrived. It's Ian Kaplan."

"You know this Ian Kaplan?" Bo asked. He heard Mattie's breath rattle, and she took a step back.

"No, but I ran a check on him as soon as he showed up," O'Malley explained. "Ian Kaplan is expensive and exclusive."

He felt another punch. That was not a good connection. So what did this exclusive lawyer have to do with a van driver with fake plates?

Bo didn't think he was going to like this answer, either.

"Do me a favor, Garrett. I told you someone's been doing computer checks on me, and it flagged firewall markers. The person used a PC in a coffeehouse over on San Pedro. I had someone lift prints from that PC, and they were running the forty or so partials they found. Is that list ready?"

Bo heard Garrett's keystrokes on the computer. "Yeah," the sergeant said a moment later. "Forty-six partials but only two hits."

The odds sucked, especially since the person responsible might not have prints on file in the database. "Is Ian Kaplan one of the hits?"

"No. But there is a name here I recognize. Kendall Collier."

Bo thought his blood might have turned to ice.

"You know, the guy that beat that illegal arms rap about a year and a half ago," Garrett continued. "His own niece testified against him, went missing and is presumed dead, but I'm thinking she went into Witness Protection and they faked her death. So why the heck would an SOB like Kendall Collier be digging into your files?"

Oh, hell.

"I'll get back to you on that," Bo told Garrett.

He shoved his phone into his pocket, caught on to Mattie's shoulders and put her hard against the wall. "I want the whole truth, and I want it *now*."

Chapter Four

Mattie wanted to give Bo the truth he was demanding, but she had no idea what that truth was. That would change. She had to figure out what was going on so she could try to keep her daughter safe.

Her daughter.

That nearly took her breath away. She was so close to her baby. Holly was just up the hall. Mattie wanted to run to her, take her and get as far away from this place as possible. But there were some big reasons why she couldn't do that.

The biggest reason now had her pressed hard against the wall.

Bo was right there, in her face, his gaze drilling into her.

"Your uncle used a computer in a coffee shop to dig into my background," Bo told her, though she didn't know how he managed to speak with his jaw that tight. "I know it was him because we found his prints on the keyboard."

It felt as if someone had punched her. "Oh, God. Kendall's closer to learning the truth than I thought. I'd hoped we'd have at least a day or two."

Bo got even closer. His chest pushed against her so that it was hard to breathe. "A day or two for what?"

"To get Holly to some place safe." Mattie mentally cursed, as well. "If Kendall used a public computer and left his fingerprints, then he wanted you to know he was searching for information on you. Have the computer checked again, because I'll bet he also used it to do searches on babies born the same day as Holly."

His eyes narrowed, his stare became even more intense, but he finally backed away from her. "Why would Kendall want me to know he's doing these things?"

"Maybe because he wants to use you to find me. So he can kill me. Of course, Kendall would never confess to something like that. According to him, he loves me and forgives me for testifying against him."

He stepped back even farther, apparently giving her theory some thought. Finally, Bo groaned and pulled out his phone again.

"Whoever you talk to," she warned, "be careful what you say."

Not that it would matter much at this point. If Kendall didn't know she was at Bo's house, then it was just a matter of time before he did. That's why she had to hurry up this conversation.

Bo dismissed her warning with an ice-cold glance with those intense brown eyes. But Mattie knew he wasn't really dismissing everything she'd just told him. No. Bo was too sensible for that. And while this had to be ripping his heart apart, he would need to get to the truth.

She was counting heavily on that.

Mattie wasn't sure who Bo reached with his call. Maybe Sergeant O'Malley again. But whoever it was, Bo requested information about her, about her Witness Protection file, and he also asked for the browsing history on the computer Kendall had used. Each request seemed to make him angrier, so Bo was in full stewing mode when he ended the call. However, she couldn't give him the time he no doubt needed to work through his anger and the bombshell she'd just delivered about being Holly's mom. They had too much to do.

"You mentioned Ian Kaplan earlier," she reminded him. "Why?"

He glared at her so long that for several moments Mattie didn't think he would answer. "He's the attorney for the guy in the black van."

Mattie's nerves had already been right at the surface, but that caused the blood to rush to her head. "Then the man in the van is connected to Kendall, because Ian is one of my uncle's lawyers."

Bo studied her. "You know this Ian?"

She nodded. "We worked together a lot when I did some P.I. jobs for my uncle. He's very loyal to Kendall. And Kendall was no doubt sending another message by having him represent the man who was probably sent here to kill me."

"You're a P.I.?" Bo questioned.

"I was. Am," she corrected, since she still had her license. "Much to the disgust of my family. The Colliers aren't big on family members with careers in law enforcement." That was a massive understatement.

"Yet your uncle hired you."

"He did. After my parents died in a car accident five years ago, Kendall sort of took me under his wing. He hired me to do background checks on potential business associates.

When I learned one of those associates was an illegal arms dealer, I told Kendall, but he didn't believe me. That's when I contacted the authorities."

"A Collier with a conscience." And it was obvious he didn't bother to tone down the sarcasm.

Mattie couldn't blame him for his attitude. He was right. Her parents had owned several investment businesses that were barely legal. She had known from an early age that they had questionable ethics, but only after she'd become a P.I. and had dug into their backgrounds had she realized just how corrupt they were.

"As you know, I testified against Kendall," she continued, "but he was acquitted."

"Because the FBI didn't have the proper search warrant when they found the incriminating documents."

She nodded, swallowed hard. "And I think because of that, Holly's father, my fiancé, was gunned down when I was six weeks pregnant. The police weren't able to find any proof of who killed him."

Bo blinked, probably because that had struck a still-raw nerve. He'd lost Nadine, the love of his life, and Mattie had lost Brody, the love of hers.

Sometimes, life just plain sucked.

"After someone tried to kidnap me," she continued, "I was placed in so-called Witness Protection. Turns out I didn't get much protection there."

Mattie took a deep breath to regain her composure, and she glanced toward the nursery. "Look, I know you have questions, but honestly they should wait."

The glare turned sharp again. "For what? For you to try to tell me again that Holly is your daughter?"

Obviously, Bo wasn't going to take her word on that, and she didn't blame him. She had walked into his ideal family life and had essentially ripped it apart.

Mattie reached into her shoulder bag. Bo reached, too, lightning fast, and he snagged her wrist.

"You already have my gun," she reminded him. Mattie waited until his grip eased a little, and she extracted the two DNA swabs that she'd bought online.

She saw the argument she and Bo were about to have, but his phone rang, cutting off the angry words that he was no doubt about to fire at her.

Bo let go of her wrist, but he stayed close, still violating her personal space. Normally,

Mattie would have put some distance between them, but she wanted to hear his phone conversation, especially when she glanced at the caller ID screen and noticed that it was Sergeant O'Malley again.

"Mattie Collier," she heard the sergeant say. "She's in Witness Protection, but someone hacked into her file. Her identity was compromised."

That didn't soften Bo's glare. "Someone tried to kill her?"

"Well, at minimum someone tried to kidnap her several times, and it's highly likely the culprit had intentions to murder her. The FBI thinks the attempts are connected to her uncle, Kendall Collier. And that brings me to the computer in the coffee shop. You wanted to know what other searches Kendall made…"

Mattie automatically moved closer, so close that her cheek brushed against the back of Bo's hand. He jerked away from her and went to the center of the room where she couldn't hear a word the sergeant was saying.

"Yeah," Bo said to the sergeant a moment later. Then the seconds crawled by. She certainly couldn't tell from Bo's expression what exactly he was being told, but she doubted it would be good news.

While he finished his conversation, Mattie

glanced out the window to make sure all was well. There were cars parked in the pristine driveways. Her own vehicle was still in front of Bo's house. Someone was walking a dog. But there were no menacing black vans or possible assassins lurking in the shadows.

Not now, anyway.

But they would come. She was certain of it.

Bo ended the call and closed his phone, but he just stood there, staring at the cell.

"You were right," he finally said. He came back across the room toward her. "Kendall used the computer to search for babies born on Holly's birthday."

Mattie wasn't exactly relieved, because it meant Kendall was closing in fast, but at least now Bo might realize that they both wanted the same thing.

To protect Holly.

"You need to know the truth about her DNA," Mattie pressed. She opened one of the kits and swabbed the inside of her mouth. She put the swab back into the plastic bag and handed it to Bo along with an unused one.

More seconds crawled by, and Mattie could feel her heart in her throat. Everything hinged on this.

Bo snatched the kits from her. "I'll have the

tests done, but I'm not giving up my daughter. Got that?"

No. She didn't get that. But now wasn't the time to argue with a father on the verge of losing a child he loved. Even if arguing was exactly what Mattie wanted to do. She wanted her baby in her arms, right here, right now. But her need for her baby would have to wait. Holly's safety had to come first, and since that safety depended on Bo's help, she had to keep this as non-hostile as possible.

"I probably don't have to remind you to keep those results a secret," she said. "Kendall has probably already bribed labs all over the city to alert him to something like this."

"I'll use the police lab," he mumbled. "And I'll make sure the results come only to me."

Well, it wasn't foolproof, especially considering how someone had hacked into her Witness Protection files, but Bo needed these test results so they could move on to the next stage. Plus, he was aware now of the danger and would hopefully be taking massive precautions.

Mattie used the pen and notepad near the house phone to jot down her number. "I obviously use a prepaid cell these days. No way to trace it. But when you find out who the man in the black van is, I'd like to know."

Bo glanced at the paper but gave her no assurance that he would do that. Mattie would give him until noon the following day. If she could wait that long. And if she hadn't heard from him, then she would call him.

"I want you to move Holly and your son to a safe house," she added. "If you can't arrange that for tonight, then ask for officers to patrol the neighborhood." She'd already noticed that he had a security system.

"Don't tell me how to protect my kids," Bo snapped. "I've done all right so far."

"Yes, but you haven't run up against the likes of my uncle."

He looked at her phone number and then the DNA kits before his gaze came back to hers. "The authorities want to talk to you."

"It'll have to wait until I can figure out a way to neutralize my uncle and his hired guns."

"Neutralize?" he repeated, sounding very much like a cop again. "What are you planning to do?"

"After I'm sure Holly is safe, I'll call Kendall and see if I can negotiate a deal with him. I'll tell him I won't testify against him if there's a new trial."

It cut her to the core to make that kind of compromise. After watching her family's dirty dealings, the one thing that Mattie had always sworn was that she wouldn't be like them. But her child was at stake. If she had any hopes of being a mother to her baby, she had to bring things to a peaceful end with Kendall.

"You believe your uncle would adhere to a truce?" Bo pressed.

"No. Not voluntarily, anyway. I plan to appeal to his new fiancée, Cicely Carr. We're old friends, and I think I can reason with her."

"And if you can't?"

Mattie met his gaze head-on. "Then I'll make arrangements to live a new life in hiding." She paused. "And then I'll petition the courts for custody of my daughter."

There. That was the gauntlet she hadn't intended to throw tonight, but a lie wouldn't have worked. Bo would have instantly spotted it and called her on it. At least this way he knew her intentions were, well, motherly.

"You're leaving now," he insisted. And to make sure that happened, he took her arm and began to haul her toward the front door.

Mattie dug in her heels and stopped, whirling around to face him. She landed against him again, body to body. They'd already touched from head to toe, so this was familiar to her now. It was almost like being in his arms.

Almost.

The seemingly permanent glare on his face didn't give her any warm and fuzzy feelings. Neither did his body for that matter. But he did stir something deep within her, and it was a stirring she preferred to ignore.

Mattie stepped back. "Please let me say good-night to Holly."

"Not a chance." He didn't roll his eyes exactly, but it was close.

It was the answer she'd expected, but it still felt like someone had clamped a fist around her heart. "You know I'm telling the truth about being her mother." Mattie didn't try to keep the emotion out of her voice, but she did try to blink back the tears.

Mattie had known she couldn't take the baby with her tonight. Well, her head had known that, anyway. The rest of her was having a hard time walking out that door even though there was no alternative. There wasn't a chance in Hades that Bo would let her leave with Holly. Not now. Probably not without a court order, which she would get.

"If you don't do the DNA test, I'll get a

judge to force you to do it," she managed to say.

But there was something new in his eyes. Something beneath the shock and the pain. Something that made her believe the test would be done. Bo was, after all, a cop, and he no doubt had a need for the truth, even if that truth was too painful to bear.

She needed the truth, too.

Mattie turned, stopped and then eased back around. This time she made sure she didn't run into him. No more touching. It was creating a warmth that shouldn't be there.

"What did Nadine say to you before she died?" Mattie asked.

The muscle in his jaw flexed again, and he glanced at the DNA baggies that he had practically crushed in his hand. "I'll call you with the test results."

Her heart suddenly felt a little lighter. It wasn't nearly as good of a concession as holding her baby would be, but it was a start.

"Your gun," he said when she started to leave. He took it from the waist of his pants and handed it to her. "You have a permit for it?"

She nodded. "Thank you—"

"Don't," he warned. "I don't want you to thank me for anything. I just want the test results to prove Holly is mine, and then I want you out of our lives forever."

Mattie nodded again. "If she's not mine, you'll never see me again." But Mattie knew the little girl was hers. Bo would soon know it, too.

She reached for the door and at the same time looked out the window. Old habits. And this time, the old habit had her hand freezing on the doorknob.

"What?" Bo snarled. But he didn't wait for her to tell him what she'd spotted. He muscled her aside and had his own look out the window.

"The dark green car," she whispered. "It's parked up the street, about fifteen feet from mine." Mattie was surprised at how calm her voice sounded when inside there was a hurricane of emotions and fear.

Especially fear.

My God. Had Kendall sent someone after her here?

"Does the car belong to one of your neighbors?" She prayed the answer would be yes, but Bo shook his head.

"Could you run the license plate?" she asked Bo, but he was already dropping the DNA bags onto the foyer table and taking out his phone.

He called someone and a moment later rattled off the plate numbers. He also drew his gun. And they stood there together while they kept watch. There was a streetlight, but because the car windows were tinted, Mattie couldn't tell if there was anyone inside. She did know the vehicle hadn't been there earlier.

"You're kidding," Bo mumbled a moment later.

His answer surprised Mattie a little, but there was certainly no humor in that remark. Worse, she saw the car door swing open.

Mattie lifted her gun and waited with her breath frozen in her lungs. The stranger kept his head down, so that she couldn't see his face. But the tall, thin man who stepped from the vehicle had dark hair.

He was also armed.

Even in the darkness she could see the familiar bulge beneath his coat.

He eased his car door shut, as if he didn't want to alert anyone to his presence, and he fired glances all around him. Mattie stepped back from the window so she'd hopefully be concealed, but she didn't take her eyes off him.

Finally, she saw his face.

And she gasped.

No. This couldn't be happening.

But that thought barely had time to register when the man whipped out a handgun. He didn't stop there.

He came straight toward the house.

Chapter Five

Bo pushed Mattie aside so he could see what had just caused her to gasp.

Hell.

A man was walking full speed ahead toward the house. Bo didn't have to guess who he was or what he wanted.

He wanted Mattie.

Bo had been able to figure that out from what Sergeant O'Malley had just told him. Now the question was, would Bo just hand her over?

As a cop, he was duty bound to do just that, but he was positive Mattie wouldn't go without a fight, and he didn't want a fight in his house with his kids just a couple of rooms away.

This was turning into being one hell of a night.

Bo positioned Mattie behind him, and he opened the door. However, he had no intention of just letting the man barge in. "The car is registered to the federal marshals," Bo let her know. "Witness Protection."

No gasp this time. Mattie groaned and no doubt understood why he'd responded with "You're kidding" when Sergeant O'Malley had told Bo about the license plates.

"I know," she mumbled.

"Larry Tolivar. U.S. Marshal," the man said, pulling back his coat so that Bo could see the badge attached to his belt.

Bo still didn't fully open the door.

"You know him?" Bo asked Mattie.

"Yes. He was the man in charge of my case. And I don't trust him."

That went without saying. Bo wasn't sure he trusted the guy either, but he didn't know exactly why.

Looking all around as if he expected an ambush, Tolivar came to a stop on the porch and reached for the door. Bo held it in place so the marshal couldn't open it any farther.

"Lieutenant Bo Duggan," he said, identifying himself. "How can I help you?"

"You can let me talk to Mattie Collier."

The guy had the attitude of a fed, all right. Some arrogance mixed with an air of authority. Well, Bo had his own damn air of authority, and he didn't exactly want to examine why he felt this stupid need to protect Mattie.

He wanted her out of his house. Away from the kids, especially Holly. And here he had the opportunity to do just that, but he couldn't forget that Mattie had nearly been kidnapped and killed while in protective custody.

"Why would you think Mattie Collier was here?" Bo demanded. It was a reasonable question, especially since he'd bet his paycheck that Mattie had taken some serious security precautions before coming to his house.

Well, he hoped she had anyway.

"She's here," Tolivar insisted. He fired another glance over his shoulder. "And you're to release her to my custody immediately."

"I'm not going with you," Mattie insisted right back.

Bo couldn't fault her for speaking up, but he would have preferred to take care of this himself. He could have sent Tolivar on his merry way and then five minutes later done the same for Mattie. Now he was in some kind of jurisdictional contest with a federal agent.

Or was he?

Tolivar had apparently been an agent at

one time, but Bo had no idea if that were still true.

Bo kept his gun ready and took out his phone again. He called Sergeant O'Malley and asked for verification. Before Tolivar could give him an outraged look, Bo used his phone to click the man's picture, and he fired the image off to O'Malley.

"Just double-checking," Bo remarked.

"Check all you want, but the bottom line is that Mattie Collier is coming with me. She's in danger and needs protection."

Mattie moved to Bo's side. "Don't make me laugh. The closest I've come to dying was when I was in your agency's custody. I entered the program voluntarily, and now I'm voluntarily leaving it."

She glanced at Bo, and the confidence that had been in her voice wasn't in her eyes. Those green eyes looked to be on the verge of spilling some tears. She also seemed to be asking for his help.

Great.

Now they were playing allies, when both of them knew they were enemies at heart.

"You can't leave the program," Tolivar insisted. "You'd be dead within an hour."

"I've done pretty well on my own for the past nineteen months."

"But there's a new threat." Tolivar huffed and switched his attention back to Bo. "You have to convince her to come with me."

"Maybe I will if you can explain how you knew she was here."

The arrogance returned to his lean expression, but then he glanced around them again. "Look, it's not a good idea to be standing out here in the open."

"Then talk fast," Bo suggested. "Because I'm not letting you in unless I have confirmation you're who you say you are." He glanced down at his phone. "No confirmation yet. So start talking."

Tolivar's mouth twisted, and he mumbled some profanity. "We've been keeping tabs on Mattie. And you."

Bo went still. "Me?"

The marshal nodded. "We were able to follow Mattie the day she went into labor. We were in the process of dispatching someone to return her to our custody and stay with her while she was in the hospital. Then the hostage situation happened, and we couldn't get to her."

"You knew I was at the hospital?" Mattie asked, her voice trembling a little now.

"We knew." No tremble for Tolivar, but he certainly wasn't as cocky as he had been earlier. Especially when his gaze came back to Bo. "We got access to the security feed, and we deduced that Mattie had been with or near your wife."

Bo let each word sink in.

"We caught just a glimpse of Mattie when she was sneaking out of the San Antonio Maternity Hospital," Tolivar continued.

"How?" Bo demanded. "Because I studied the surveillance tapes, and I didn't see when or where she left the building."

Tolivar glanced away. "I was there, and we had several agents watching. We thought she might try to get out before anyone could find her. And we were right. We got just a glimpse of her coming out of the service entrance."

Bo shook his head. "The cops were watching that entrance."

"Not by then. The gunman had just driven off with a hostage, and most of the other officers, including you, had raced into the building."

Later, Bo would make this moron give an official statement as to why a federal marshal had seen a possible witness escape and hadn't alerted the police.

"As I said, we got just a glimpse of Mattie as she was leaving, but we lost her soon afterward," Tolivar added. "And because we didn't know where she'd gone, we kept looking for flags. You, Lieutenant, were one of those flags."

That hung in the air a few seconds before it hit Bo like a heavyweight's fist. Mattie had a similar reaction, because she gasped and elbowed her way in front of Bo.

"Are you saying—" But she couldn't finish.

Bo, however, could finish. He pushed Mattie back behind him and grabbed on to Tolivar's lapels, pulling the man closer so that Bo was right in his face.

"You knew Mattie had been in the room with my wife?" Bo clarified, though he couldn't stop the anger from raging through him.

"We deduced it after reading through all the notes of the investigation and eyewitness reports." Tolivar's breathing suddenly became uneven. "We knew Mattie and your wife had been in labor rooms next to each other and that they disappeared before the gunmen could round them up with the other hostages. We didn't know exactly what went on between the women, but we thought that eventually Mattie would come to you. Maybe because of something that…happened when she was with your wife."

Bo had to get his teeth unclenched. "Say it, you SOB. Say that you knew Mattie was pregnant when she went in the hospital but didn't have a baby with her when she came out. Say it!"

"We didn't know for sure what had happened," Tolivar insisted.

But they sure as hell had guessed. "You waited, watching, for her to come to me."

Tolivar didn't deny it, and even if he had, Bo wouldn't have believed him. He cursed and wanted to ram his fist into this man's face. And he might have done just that if Mattie hadn't pulled him back. She couldn't have done that unless Bo had allowed it, but he was so riled that he didn't trust himself to settle for just one punch. He wanted to clean his porch with this guy.

"Just leave," Mattie told the marshal.

Good idea. That way, Bo could try to deal with what he had just learned. Hell. Everything he'd believed about the past thirteen months had been a lie.

Tolivar shook his head. "I can't leave, not until I convince you to come with me."

"You're wasting your breath," she assured him. She reached for the door to slam it shut.

"There's an assassin after you," Tolivar said, blocking her attempt to shut the door.

"Tell me something I don't know." And Mattie tried to shut the door again.

"An assassin who was hired today," Tolivar continued. "This afternoon, as a matter of fact. We have reason to believe he knows about your connection to the lieutenant."

Bo just stared at the man and didn't know whether to laugh or curse again.

Mattie's gaze met Bo's, and he saw the fight in her eyes turn to pure, raw frustration. "I'm sorry. I didn't know."

"And you still don't," Bo quickly assured her. "The marshal here could have made up the assassin story to get you to go with him."

Why the heck he was volunteering that, Bo didn't know. He probably needed his head examined, but by God, he didn't want this swaggering fed to ride roughshod over a woman who had already had enough people run over her.

While he was at it, Bo decided this bozo could be lying about the baby situation, as well. He didn't believe anything that came out of Tolivar's mouth.

"You'll be sorry, and dead, if you don't come back into our protection," Tolivar warned Mattie.

That was the last straw. Bo slammed the

door in the marshal's face, locked it and set the security system.

"Is everything okay?" Rosalie called out.

Since Bo didn't know the answer, he settled for saying, "Just stay put. I'll be in there soon."

First, he had to figure out how to diffuse a very big bomb.

Bo kept an eye on Tolivar. The marshal did indeed return to his vehicle, and he sped away. Bo didn't think for one minute that this was the last they would see of him. Tolivar would likely go to his office and return with backup.

Well, maybe.

Legally, there was no way anyone in Witness Protection could force Mattie to return, since she wasn't under any obligation to testify. But that meant Bo had to figure out what to do with her.

"Keep an eye out. See if Tolivar comes back," Bo told Mattie.

She went over to the window, freeing him to keep an eye on the area where his children were. He also took out his phone, and this time he called his boss, Captain Shaw Tolbert. Since Shaw's own wife had also been a maternity hostage, the captain had personal knowledge of what had gone on that day.

Hopefully, not too personal.

Hell. No one in SAPD better have known about Mattie leaving her baby behind while she went on the run.

"Bo," Shaw answered, obviously seeing his name on the caller ID. "I just got a call from a marshal over in Witness Protection."

They worked fast, and that meant Bo had to play catch-up. "Mattie Collier," Bo started. He walked down the hall toward the nursery. "She's here at my house. You happen to know why?"

"If I'm to believe what Marshal Tolivar said, Mattie gave birth to a baby girl and left the newborn with Nadine." The captain paused. "Is it true?"

Bo cracked open the nursery door and peered inside. Rosalie was seated in the rocking chair and had a baby in the crook of each arm, much the way Nadine had been holding them when Bo had found her in the nurses' lounge after the end of the hostage incident.

Rosalie glanced up but continued to read a Dr. Seuss book to Jacob and Holly. There was nothing unusual about that. Rosalie and Bo both read to them a lot. It was part of their nightly routine.

Tonight, it caused his heart to ache.

He'd taken moments like this for granted.

He had thought that because he'd endured Nadine's death, there wouldn't be any more nightmares to face.

Well, he might be facing one now.

He couldn't lose his little girl. He just couldn't. It would be like losing Nadine all over again.

"Bo?" the captain said. "Is it true?"

"I'm not sure," he whispered. Bo stepped back and closed the door so his conversation wouldn't disturb story time or alarm Rosalie.

That obviously wasn't the answer Shaw wanted to hear, because he cursed. "What do you want to do about it?"

Nothing. Bo wanted to send Mattie on her way and pretend this night had never happened. But he couldn't do that. Damn it. He couldn't live his life with his head in the sand, even if that's exactly what he wanted to do right now.

"Mattie just gave me a sample of her DNA," Bo continued. "I can use the cheek swab on Holly. The samples need to be compared."

Compared. That was such a benign word for something that could change his and his family's lives forever.

"I'll have someone pick up the samples tonight," Shaw concluded. "I can log them in under my name so that it won't be connected to you or Mattie. The lab will put a rush on them, and you should know something by tomorrow."

Bo didn't thank his captain because the words would have stuck in his throat. He was already dreading that the tests had to be run, but what he was dreading more were the results.

He took a deep breath to try to steady his knotted stomach, and Bo forced his mind back on the next task at hand. Mattie was still by the front window, and she was volleying glances outside and at him.

What are you going to do? she seemed to be asking.

Bo was wondering the same thing.

"If Tolivar is telling the truth, then there's an assassin after Mattie," Bo informed the captain.

"It's possible. I've been checking her records while we've been talking, and while she was in Witness Protection, her identity was compromised."

"How?" Bo wanted to know. "And who did it?"

"As for the how, someone hacked into the computer database. They don't know who was responsible, but the department believes this goes back to Mattie's uncle, Kendall Collier."

Yeah. He certainly had the most to gain by finding her.

Revenge.

God knows what Collier would be prepared to do to find a niece who had, in his mind, betrayed him.

"Collier's a rich, powerful man," Bo pointed out. "Is it possible he has this Marshal Tolivar on his payroll?"

"It's possible. It would have taken money and resources to hack into the Witness Protection database. Collier has the money, and Tolivar has the resources." Shaw's quick response meant he'd already thought of it. "Let me handle looking into that. In the meantime, we have this situation with Miss Collier."

Yeah, it was a situation, all right. She was looking at him with those sad doe eyes again.

"Mattie needs to be in protective custody," Shaw added.

Bo snapped back his shoulders. "You aren't suggesting we turn her over to Witness Protection."

"No. Besides, I doubt she'd be too eager to go with them."

"You're right about that." It was stupid to

feel even mildly relieved that she wouldn't go back into a system that had nearly gotten her killed. "So, what do we do with her?"

"We protect her," Shaw simply stated. "She did law enforcement a huge favor by testifying against her uncle, and it wasn't her fault that the FBI screwed up the search warrant and got most of their evidence thrown out."

No. It wasn't her fault. And it wasn't his that this mess had been brought right to his home.

"What are you suggesting?" Bo asked.

"Probably something you don't want to do, but hear me out, Bo. Mattie Collier is already there, and until I can make other arrangements, that's the safest place for her."

There went another shot of adrenaline and anger. Because so many objections came to mind, it took Bo a moment to pick which one to verbalize first. "There's an assassin after her and maybe even a corrupt federal marshal. My kids are here in the house."

"Yeah. I know, and as a dad myself, I know your twins are your first priority. That includes Holly."

That knot in his stomach twisted and tightened. Bo knew what the captain meant. If Collier, the assassin or anyone else after Mattie suspected that Holly was her daughter, they might try to take his little girl to get Mattie to cooperate.

Hell.

It wouldn't even have to be true that Mattie was Holly's biological mother. The SOBs would just have to think that it was.

When he looked at Mattie this time, he was sure his eyes were narrowed to slits. How dare she bring this danger right to his babies.

She shook her head, obviously not understanding the venom he was now aiming at her.

"What are you asking me to do?" Bo questioned the captain. And he held his breath, waiting for the other shoe to fall.

"I'll get to work on a safe house, one under our jurisdiction. One where I can control the security until we can get this all figured out. I would move you now, but this is going to require a lot of work to make sure we're not taking you from the frying pan and into the fire. I want to make the arrangements myself and keep it out of anyone else's hands. Until I can work out everything, I'll send a couple of officers to sit in front of your place in a patrol car. That should deter an assassin or anyone else."

"You're sure about that?" Bo managed to say.

The captain paused. "I'll make things as

safe for your family as possible. But in the meantime, Mattie Collier stays there, with you, in *your* protective custody."

Chapter Six

Protective custody.

To Mattie, this arrangement didn't feel so protective, not with Bo's obvious disapproval at her presence in his house. He had made her feel totally unwelcome, and it had started before the conversation with his captain had even ended.

After that call, Bo had grumbled that she would be staying at his house for the night, and then he'd promptly disappeared into the nursery, leaving Rosalie to show Mattie to the guest room. Rosalie had relayed Bo's order for Mattie to stay put in the guest room until morning. In other words, he didn't want her sneaking out to look at Holly.

Of course, she couldn't blame Bo and Rosalie for the chilly reception. Mattie had made a massive mistake by coming to Bo's.

But then, maybe not.

If Kendall had suspected that Holly was her

baby, then it was just a matter of time before he would have used the child to get to her.

That didn't make Mattie feel any better.

Her baby was still in danger, and even though she might be one step closer to proving that Holly was hers, what good would that do unless she could neutralize the danger?

As she'd done many times over the past year and a half, she wished Kendall were in jail where he couldn't be as much of a threat. But since he wasn't, that meant Mattie had to deal with the devil himself. She had to call Kendall and try to negotiate a deal with him.

Her life for Holly's safety.

Of course, there were no guarantees that Kendall would agree or, even if he did, that he would abide by any agreement with her. Plus, Mattie didn't want to die. She had been on the run for so long that fighting for her life was as natural as breathing. Still, if it came down to it, she would turn herself over to Kendall for a guaranteed assurance that Holly would be okay.

Mattie glanced at the clock on the nightstand next to the bed. It was 5:00 a.m. She'd gotten maybe an hour's sleep, and with every sound she heard, she'd reached for her gun. Bo had no doubt done the same, especially since he'd spent the night in the nursery. She knew this because the guest room was next to the nursery, and before the babies had fallen asleep, she'd heard Bo playing with them. She hadn't heard the door open or him walk out.

The sounds of Holly's laughter had filled Mattie with more love than she could have ever imagined. It had also caused her heart to ache. She had missed so much already. Thirteen months was a lifetime when it came to a baby. And her little girl was no longer a newborn but a toddler learning to walk.

Mattie hated Kendall for taking that time away from her.

She glanced at the clock again and groaned softly. A whole two minutes had passed. She wanted the hour to fly by because the quicker the time passed, the sooner she might get to see Holly. Of course, Bo might continue to lock all three of them in the nursery. Or he might usher Mattie out of his house as soon as it was daylight. He wasn't just going to hand over Holly without some kind of court order.

Mattie threw back the covers and got up, since it was obvious she wasn't going to fall back asleep. She took off the loaner gown that Rosalie had given her so she could dress in the green pants and top she'd worn the day before. Since she didn't have a change of clothes, she'd washed her underwear the night before and had hung it on the chair to dry. Her bra was still damp, but it would have to do. At least she had a toothbrush and some toiletries in her bag. Along with her gun.

Being on the run had taught her to be prepared.

Mattie didn't really need to use the bathroom because she'd gotten up just about an hour earlier to do that, but she did need to brush her teeth and freshen up. She grabbed her purse and threw open the door so she could head to the bathroom just up the hall. She didn't get far. She turned and smacked right into Bo.

Suddenly, she was smothered in his arms and against his chest. It didn't take but a split second to register that those arms and chest were bare and that there was a warm, male, musky scent to go along with all those toned muscles.

"Oh," she managed to say, and she stepped back. But it was already too late. That scent and touch had gotten to her and had seeped right into her body, warming her in places that shouldn't be warm.

Not when it came to Bo, anyway.

Mattie soon realized that touching him was

off-limits, but seeing him had the same effect on her. His hair was rumpled, as if he'd just climbed out of bed.

After a long night of sex.

His five-o'clock shadow was now more outlaw stubble. Dark and dangerous. Like the man himself. He wore loose jeans that were slung low on his hips, and it gave her a nice view of the abs to go along with the rest of his nearly perfect body.

Perfect except for the scar on his right shoulder.

It looked like a gunshot wound. And that snapped her out of the hot-body fantasy she was weaving around him.

"What are you doing up?" he growled.

His tone further dampened her fantasy, even though being near him had a unique way of renewing that fantasy.

"I couldn't sleep," she whispered and glanced over his shoulder. The nursery door was closed. "Thank God we had a quiet night." Quiet as in no one had attempted to kill them.

Bo made a sound that was minimally agreeable. "They're still in bed," he grumbled, obviously following her gaze.

Hopefully he hadn't followed her gaze when she'd given his body the once-over. But he obviously had. Mattie realized that when their eyes met. She didn't have a ton of experience with men, but she saw the glimmer of heat.

Involuntary heat, that is.

Bo's mouth turned to a snarl, but even that didn't make him less hot.

"Sorry," he mumbled at the exact moment that Mattie said the same.

They stared at each other, apparently waiting to see which would be the first to put a foot in their mouth.

Mattie decided to go first. "Don't worry. Even if we didn't have some huge obstacles between us, you're not my type."

The corner of his mouth lifted, but it was just as much a snarl as a smile. "Yeah. I'm a cop, and you're from a family of criminals."

She winced before she could hide her reaction. It stung. Always did when people linked her to her scummy family.

"Sorry," he mumbled again.

She tried to shrug. "I did voluntarily go to work for my uncle," Mattie admitted. "So, I deserve that."

He shook his head and mumbled something under his breath. "No. You didn't." Bo motioned toward the kitchen. "Want some coffee?"

She did, desperately. Her brain was screaming for a caffeine fix. But her gaze wandered back to the nursery.

"They won't be up for another half hour or so," Bo let her know. "Rosalie's in there with them now."

Good. So the babies weren't alone. Even though Rosalie had assured her the windows were wired to the security system, Mattie still didn't want to take any chances. If someone tried to break into the nursery, Rosalie would be there to get the children out.

Mattie followed him into the kitchen, placed her purse on the counter and sat at the table while Bo started the coffee. He then disappeared into the adjoining laundry room and a few seconds later came out wearing a snug black T-shirt. End of the peep show, which was just as well.

"So, why did you go to work for your uncle?" he asked. He opened the fridge and took out the makings for breakfast. Eggs, bacon and orange juice.

Mattie's stomach growled, and she realized it'd been noon the day before since she'd eaten. Would Bo let her stay for breakfast, or would he have her out of there before the kids woke up? It wasn't even 5:30 yet, but she had no idea how long Holly and Jacob would stay asleep.

When he glanced back at her, Mattie realized he was waiting for an answer to his question.

"Kendall talked me into coming to work for him, after he'd assured me that he was nothing like my father. He offered me a great salary with medical insurance. Since my fiancé and I were planning on having a child, I thought it was a good idea." She paused. "I obviously thought wrong. My father was a saint compared to Kendall."

Bo made another of those sounds, a cross between agreement and a male grunt, and he poured her a cup of coffee, sliding it across the table toward her.

Since this was the most civil he had been to her, Mattie hated to ruin the moment, but they had things to discuss.

"Did you send the DNA tests to the lab?" she asked.

He froze a moment, turned his back to her and started to make the bacon and eggs. "Captain Shaw had an officer pick up the samples last night."

And that was apparently all Bo intended to volunteer.

"Holly's DNA will be a match to mine," Mattie continued, knowing she was wading into deep, dangerous waters.

He didn't issue one of those grunts this time, but he did aim a glare at her from over his shoulder.

"We've identified the man who was in the black van," he said, obviously ignoring her assertion that the DNA tests would match. "His name is Terrance Arturo. You know him?"

She repeated the name to see if it would jog any memories. It didn't. "No. He works for Kendall?"

"We're not sure. His lawyer hasn't allowed him to say much."

Yes, his lawyer. "Ian Kaplan."

"Just how well do you know him?" Bo pressed.

"I worked with him for months, but I knew him before that. I thought he was a decent guy." Mattie paused again. "I think he had a crush on me or something, because he seemed to be jealous of Brody, my late fiancé."

Now she got a grunt. And silence. The only sound came from the sizzling bacon.

"Nadine said you were, and I quote, 'the best husband in the world.'" Mattie waited for a response but didn't get one. Bo continued to beat the eggs that he'd just cracked into a small bowl. "She talked about you almost the whole time she was in labor."

Even through his T-shirt, she saw the

muscles in his back tense. "Did she blame me for not being there to rescue her?"

Oh. So, that's what was going on in his mind. "No. Just the opposite. She insisted that you would come for her. And you did."

"Too little, too late," he mumbled. He set aside the eggs he'd been beating as if they were suddenly too fragile to be in his hands, probably because he had a death grip on the glass bowl. Then he turned around to face her.

"Not too late for Jacob and Holly," Mattie insisted. "And as for Nadine, that wasn't your fault."

"The hell it wasn't." His gaze fired all around the room as if he were looking for someplace to aim the dangerous energy that was a powder keg inside him.

It was a massive risk, but Mattie got up and walked over to him. "Despite the circumstances, Nadine was happy when she gave birth to your son." She reached out, touched his arm.

Bo jerked away from her at first, but when Mattie caught his wrist, he didn't fight it. He just stared at her, and she could see and feel every ounce of the pain that he was experiencing.

"Nadine knew she was going to die?" he asked, his voice barely a whisper.

Mattie shook her head. "I'm not sure." She inched even closer and blinked back the tears that were burning her eyes. "She said you were the love of her life. The answer to her prayers. She also said you would help me."

Now he tried to pull away, but Mattie held on. "I need your help, Bo. I need you to tell me what Nadine said when you got to her in the nurses' lounge."

For a moment, she thought that was the end of their conversation. He was putting up that wall again. But then, something changed. Bo didn't dodge her gaze. Instead, he looked deep into her eyes.

She was aware of the sounds. The smells. The bacon was either burning or close to it. But the only thing she saw was Bo.

A raw groan tore from his throat, and he pulled her to him, against him. Not a punishing grip. A hug. He pulled her into his arms.

"Nadine said, 'We have to protect her.' And then she closed her eyes and didn't open them again."

"Her," Mattie repeated. "Nadine meant Holly. I told her to ask you to protect my baby."

She held her breath, waiting for Bo to admit that Holly was hers, but the sounds stopped him from saying anything.

It was a giggle. Followed by footsteps.

Bo jerked away from her and moved the bacon off the burner. He pushed past her and headed for the hall just as Jacob rounded the corner. He was wearing only a diaper and a single blue sock.

Even though the little boy was obviously a novice at walking, he was doing a good job making his way to his dad. He had a big grin on his face as if he'd just done something naughty but fun. Mattie found herself smiling despite the tense, heart-wrenching conversation she'd just had with Bo.

"Jacob?" Rosalie called out. "Get back in here."

The little boy giggled and made a beeline for his father. Bo scooped him up his arms and gave him a kiss on the cheek. "Did you escape?"

Jacob babbled something the two males must have understood, because they shared a grin.

A moment later, a harried-looking Rosalie appeared in the doorway. But Mattie's heart sank, because Holly wasn't with her.

"That boy's getting faster every day,"

Rosalie complained, laughing. "And they both got up way too early this morning."

"Go ahead and tend to Holly," Bo told her. "I'll get Jacob some breakfast."

Jacob's attention landed on Mattie, and he reached for her. "Tiss," he insisted.

Mattie was certain she looked confused, but before she could ask what the little boy wanted, Jacob shifted his weight and practically plunged into her arms.

"Tiss," Jacob repeated, and he gave her a kiss on the end of her nose.

For such a simple gesture, it filled her with more emotion than she would have thought possible. Mattie felt the tears threaten again.

So this was what it was like to have a child.

"Jacob obviously likes to kiss," Bo mumbled, and he pulled out one of the two high chairs that were stored against the wall. "And run around half naked. Come on, son. Time to eat."

That got Jacob's attention, and he went right back to Bo so his dad could put him in the high chair. Bo sprinkled some dry cereal O's right onto the tray and went back to finish the scrambled eggs.

Bo's cell phone rang, and he pulled it from his pocket and sandwiched the phone between his ear and shoulder so he could continue to cook. His motions were seamless. He'd obviously fallen right into the daddy routine.

"He wants what?" Bo asked, causing Mattie to walk closer. His body language suddenly indicated there was a problem. "You've got to be kidding me."

Mattie tried to listen to the conversation, but it was drowned out by the sound of Rosalie's voice. The nanny was talking to Holly, and she walked into the kitchen with the little girl in her arms.

Mattie froze, unable to take her eyes off the child. Yes, she'd seen her the night before, but not this close. So close she could finally touch those curls. And that's exactly what Mattie tried to do. But unlike Jacob, Holly pulled back, burying her face against Rosalie's neck.

"She's shy around strangers," Rosalie remarked, and the nanny looked to Bo for what appeared to be some kind of approval. But Bo was caught up in his phone call.

Mattie figured that call was important, but she couldn't take her attention off her daughter. She reached out, hoping that Holly would have a change of heart and come to her, but the baby shook her head and grumbled, "No."

Jacob, however, wanted her attention, and he grabbed Mattie's hand, turning her toward him. He held out one of the cereal bits for her to take. She did, and that earned her one of those grins from the little boy.

"Everything okay?" Rosalie asked Bo the moment he ended the call. The nanny put Holly in the high chair next to Jacob.

"I'm not sure." Bo shook his head, and he glanced at Mattie before heading out of the kitchen and into the living room. "Ian Kaplan is out front, and he wants to see you."

"What?" Mattie raced after him and went to the sidelight window of the front door. The sun was just beginning to rise, but there was enough light for her to spot the blond-haired man leaning against the pricey red sports car.

It was Ian, all right.

"How did he even know I was here?" she asked.

Bo walked to her side and stared out the window with her. "He won't tell the officers that."

Mattie was betting either Kendall told him or else Ian had learned it from his new client, Terrance Arturo, the guy in the black van.

"Ian wanted me to give you a message,"

Bo continued. "He says he can save your life, and all you have to do is walk out there and talk to him."

Chapter Seven

Walk out there and talk to him.

Right. As if Bo would let that happen. But one glance at Mattie, and he knew she was considering it.

"Ian could gun you down on the way out the door," Bo reminded her.

"The two officers are out there. I doubt they'd let him pull a gun." However, she didn't sound completely convinced of that.

Bo tried again. "I don't want to risk a shootout with my kids in the house."

Since he was trying to reason with her, he probably should have said *the* kids instead of *my* kids, but the truth was, they were his. Both of them. And that didn't have anything to do with DNA. It made his heart ache just thinking of the possibility that he might lose a child he loved more than life itself.

Of course, Mattie no doubt loved Holly, too.

Still, Mattie hadn't raised Holly for the past

thirteen months. She had no history with the baby. She only had a mountain of danger that might fall down on her at any minute. And because of that danger, Bo needed to move Jacob and Holly as soon as he got Ian away from the house.

"But what if Ian can put an end to this mess?" Mattie asked.

Bo took out his phone and pressed in the number to the officers out front. "Then he can tell you all about it while he's out there and you're in here."

"Let me speak to our visitor," Bo told the officer when he answered, and he watched as the young cop did just that.

"Lieutenant Duggan," Ian spat out, making it sound like profanity. "I want to see Mattie."

Bo moved Mattie in front of the sidelight window for just a second and then pulled her back. "There, you've seen her. Now, tell me how you knew she was here."

Ian flashed a snarky smile. "Well, the cops in front of your house were a dead giveaway."

"Wrong answer." Bo put some snark in his voice. "Try again."

That at least wiped the smile off Ian's face. "Look, Mattie and I are on the same side here. I just want to make sure she's safe."

"She is. And you dodged the question again. How did you know she was here?"

Definitely no smile now. The man's eyes narrowed. "Put Mattie on the phone, and I'll tell her."

Bo merely clicked on the speaker function. "She's listening."

"Mattie," Ian said after several seconds. "I want to talk to you *in private*."

She looked up at Bo, and he shook his head.

"Ian, what is this all about?" Mattie asked. "Why are you here?"

"Why?" he snapped as if the answer were obvious. "Because I care about you. Because I want to keep you alive. I can do that, Mattie. All you have to do is talk to me."

"I will…if you'll tell me how you knew I was here."

Good for her. Because Bo was certain that information would give him some critical details about Ian—like his motive for this untimely visit.

Ian huffed and shook his head before he responded. "I hired Terrance Arturo to find you."

Mattie's mouth dropped open. "The man in the van that you're representing?"

"Yes. He's not exactly a P.I., but he's done

this sort of work for me before. And for the record, he didn't know about the phony plates on the van. He borrowed the vehicle from a friend."

Bo figured that would be easy enough to confirm. "But how did Arturo find Mattie? She's been in hiding."

More hesitation. "Arturo found Mattie through you."

Mattie pressed her fingers to her lips, and groaned softly.

"Explain that," Bo demanded.

"I've been trying to find Mattie all this time, and I hired several people to look for her. I figured she might visit her old friends. Or Brody's grave." Ian paused again. "I also anticipated that she might want to talk to you, since Mattie and your wife were in the hospital the day the maternity hostages were taken. Mattie's got a good heart, and she probably wanted to tell you about your wife's last hours. Am I right?"

Bo didn't answer.

"I mean, why else would she have gone to you?" Ian added. Maybe he was faking it, but there didn't seem to be any smugness in that remark. "I also had some of the other hostages and the nurses from the hospital followed. I figured it was one of the nurses who'd taken Mattie's baby."

Interesting theory, especially since that had happened with one of the other hostages. But did Ian believe that had also happened with Mattie's newborn, or was Ian's explanation designed to try to put Mattie more at ease?

Bo didn't care right now. He only wanted this man away from his home.

"Marshal Larry Tolivar also helped me find Mattie," Ian commented.

That grabbed Bo's attention. "Helped how?"

"Inadvertently." Ian's smiled returned. "The marshal was pressing any- and everyone who knew Mattie to give up her whereabouts, so I figured he'd find her. So, I had him followed, as well."

That was a lot of time and manpower to locate Mattie.

"How can you save my life?" Mattie asked. She glanced over her shoulder when she heard Holly start to fuss. Bo knew that whine. Rosalie was likely wiping the baby's face. But it obviously spiked Mattie's nerves.

"I'll tell you that when I can actually see you," Ian insisted.

Bo was tired of this game and decided to

put an end to it. "Mattie and I will meet you at police headquarters. You can tell her there."

He saw the flash of surprise in Ian's expression, and he expected the lawyer to turn him down flat. But Ian checked his watch. "How soon?" Ian pressed.

"An hour." Bo looked at Mattie, and she agreed with a nod.

"I'll be there." Ian turned as if to get back into his vehicle but then stopped. "Mattie, don't go on the run again. It's not necessary. I've worked out a deal for you. A deal that will keep you safe." Ian handed the phone back to the officer, got in his car and drove away.

"A deal," Mattie repeated. She looked both hopeful and frightened. After all the attempts that had been made to get to her, Bo understood the reaction.

He also understood what he had to do. He ended the call and called his captain. Yes, it was early, but this was too important to wait.

"Tell Rosalie to get the kids dressed and ready to leave," he instructed Mattie.

Mattie must have wholeheartedly agreed with that request because she hurried away. Or maybe she was just anxious to get back in the room with Holly.

"One of the officers at your house just gave me an update," the captain greeted him.

"Yeah. Ian Kaplan was here. Mattie and I are meeting with him at headquarters in one hour. But I want to move the kids before we go."

Bo walked back to the kitchen, where Mattie was trying to coax Holly from Rosalie's arms. Holly would have no part of it, so Mattie ended up taking Jacob from the high chair instead. His son gave Mattie a *tiss* and wound his arms around her neck.

"I thought you'd want the twins away from there," Shaw answered. "So, here's what I need you to do. The two officers at your house will take your nanny, Jacob and Holly to my house. I'm here and I'll stay here for at least the next two hours. Then, Mattie and you can meet with Ian Kaplan. If nothing is resolved in that meeting, then we can work out a protective custody arrangement for Mattie and the kids if necessary."

Oh, it would unfortunately be necessary.

"My advice?" Shaw continued. "Get the kids and Rosalie out of there quickly. If we're really dealing with Kendall Collier, then it's best to start putting up some buffers."

Bo couldn't agree more.

"One more thing," Shaw said before Bo

could hang up. "Those DNA test results should be done soon."

Great. Something else to deal with, and the results could be as potentially dangerous as an assassin after Mattie.

Bo ended the call and hurried to the garage so he could open it for the officers. He tossed one of them the keys to the white SUV that Rosalie used. "You'll need to move the infant seats into your patrol car," he instructed. There was a set of seats in both his and Rosalie's vehicles, but the ones in the white SUV were easier to remove.

Bo hurried back to the nursery so he could help Rosalie and Mattie. But the women already had it under control. Mattie was dressing Jacob in denim overalls and a shirt. For once, his son was actually cooperating with the dressing process and was babbling away to Mattie.

Mattie looked up, snagged Bo's gaze. "Where will you take them?"

"The officers will take Rosalie and them to the captain's house."

Rosalie did the snaps on Holly's pink overalls. "I'm guessing this is necessary?" the nanny asked.

"It is." Bo put his phone in his pocket so he could take Jacob from Mattie.

"Because of me," Mattie mumbled. "Bo, I'm so sorry—"

"Don't." And because he sounded so gruff, he toned it down a little. "I believe both Marshal Tolivar and Kendall Collier have been watching me. Eventually, this would have happened."

"Maybe not. If I hadn't shown up…"

Then, Collier might have used Holly to get to Mattie. Of course, that left Bo with a big question—why hadn't Collier tried to use Holly sooner?

Maybe the man hadn't known about Holly's possible connection to Mattie after all? And maybe there was no connection. Maybe the DNA test would prove it. If so, Bo could put an end to the danger and the custody threat in one fell swoop. Mattie could then be on her way to locate her own child.

So why didn't that feel as perfect a scenario as it should have?

Maybe because of that pained look on Mattie's face. She was obviously hurting, and Bo was hurting for her. He wasn't cold and heartless, and with Mattie around, he was getting a constant reminder of the camaraderie that was starting between them.

And of the attraction.

It was there, simmering, creating all sorts of problems for him.

Rosalie grabbed the diaper bag and looped it over her shoulder. Since there was no reason to delay things, Bo took a deep breath and headed for the garage.

"Let's make this quick," he instructed while they were still in the cover of the garage. "I don't want the kids out in the open any longer than necessary."

The officers pulled up into the driveway, directly behind the SUVs, and they opened the doors.

Bo gave Jacob a kiss on the cheek. "Be a good boy," Bo told him. And he pulled Holly into his other arm so he could kiss her, as well.

"Da Da," Holly said, and then poked out her bottom lip as if she might burst into tears. His baby girl did not like to have her routine broken, and she probably sensed that something wasn't quite right.

Bo handed Jacob over to Rosalie, giving him a moment to console Holly.

"It's okay," he whispered to Holly, and he kissed her again. Bo pulled her closer for a hug, and her little arms coiled around his neck. "Daddy will be back soon."

When Bo glanced at Mattie, he saw the

tears in her eyes. He mentally groaned. This goodbye was just as hard for her as it was for him.

"Why don't you say bye-bye to Mattie?" Bo prompted the little girl.

Holly's big green eyes were suddenly curious, and she even managed a slight smile as she waved. "Bye-bye, Ma."

That *Ma* was obviously Holly's attempt to say Mattie's name, but it caused the moment to freeze. Mattie reached for her as if she might yank her right out of Bo's arms. But she didn't. Mattie's hands fell back to her side, and the smile she gave Holly would have melted a heart of stone.

"They should go," Mattie said, though there was little sound to her words.

She turned and went back into the house before Bo could even attempt to comfort her. Which was just as well. He didn't know what to say or do to make this better. Besides, he needed to get the kids out of there.

He took the lead, heading to the passenger's side of the car with Holly. Rosalie went to the other side, and they strapped the twins into the car seats. Rosalie took the seat between them.

"I'll call you after the meeting at headquarters," Bo assured the nanny, and then he kissed the babies one more time.

This wasn't an ordinary goodbye, but he prayed it wouldn't be a long one. He needed the twins far more than they needed him.

Bo stepped back into the garage and watched as they drove away. He waited until the patrol car was out of sight before he closed the garage door and went back inside, expecting to see Mattie.

But he didn't.

He heard the sound of water running and followed it until he found her. She was in the bathroom, door open, and she was brushing her teeth. Her movements were frantic, probably because her hands were shaking.

"I'll do whatever it takes in this meeting to get this all resolved," she promised. She grabbed a brush from her purse and assaulted her hair with it.

Bo went to her, took the brush from her hand. Or rather tried to. She fought him, struggling to hang on to it, all the while tears pooling in her eyes. He could feel the nervous energy radiating from her.

He gave up on the brush and hauled her into his arms.

Mattie put up a token resistance. And then fell apart. The sobs racked through her, consuming her, and Bo knew there was nothing he could say or do except stand there and let her cry it out.

He wasn't sure how long the worst of it lasted, minutes probably, but each minute drilled home that this situation with Mattie was not going to be resolved easily. Somehow, in this already dangerous mix, Bo had started to be concerned about her. Not her situation.

But *her*.

Maybe that had something to do with the way Jacob had taken to her. Or maybe it was this stupid attraction.

As if she'd read his mind, Mattie lifted her head and looked into his eyes. They were too close, of course, because she was in his arms. Her breath met his, and he drew her scent and taste into his mouth.

Oh, man.

He didn't want this.

But apparently the warning wasn't enough, because he lowered his head and kissed her. Bo instantly changed his mind.

He wanted this.

Her mouth was damp from her tears, and he could taste the salt and her mint toothpaste. That should have been a turnoff, a big red flag that the timing sucked for kissing, but it didn't turn off anything for him. Bo kissed her, keeping it soft and gentle, so he could take in everything her mouth was telling him.

And what her mouth was saying was that she wanted this, too.

Mattie made a soft sound deep within her throat. Part surprise, part pleasure. Almost hesitantly, she put her hands on his chest. First one, then the other. She leaned into him, closer and closer, increasing the pressure of the kiss with each fraction of distance that she erased between them.

The pressure erased the soft and gentle approach, too, and Bo found himself taking rather than consoling. Her taste hit him like a ton of bricks. It had been so long since he'd kissed a woman and had one in his arms that his body was suddenly greedy for more.

He took more.

Bo deepened the kiss, touching his tongue to hers.

The jolt hit him even harder. Man, this was not a good place to go with a very vulnerable woman who had more emotional baggage than he did.

Mattie obviously realized that, too, because she jerked back, an "oh" rushing from her mouth as she took her lips from his. She blinked, stared up at him and repeated the "oh."

Bo repeated it, too. "Sorry," he said, because he didn't have a clue what else to say. Kissing Mattie was wrong on too many levels to count. He pushed aside the part about how right it'd felt, though.

She fluttered her fingers in the direction of the bathroom. "We should, uh, finish dressing so we can leave for the meeting with Ian."

Yeah, they should. And they would once he could walk. That kiss had aroused him beyond belief.

"What do you think Ian is going to say to you?" Bo asked, hoping a real conversation would get his mind off that kiss and the hard ache in his body.

She shook her head. "I'm not sure. I've had a mixed experience with Ian. After Brody was killed, Ian offered to have me move in with him so he could help me raise the baby I was carrying. I obviously turned him down."

"How did he take that?"

"With cool anger," she readily answered. "I mean, I knew he was upset, but he stayed polite. Why?"

"Just trying to get a handle on what we're dealing with here." And since his thoughts were more sexual than business, Bo moved away from her. "I'll get dressed."

Bo moved but then stopped. "Do we need to talk about what just happened?"

"No." She answered so quickly that it left no room for argument.

Which was a good thing in his mind. Because the kiss shouldn't have happened in the first place. And it wouldn't happen again.

Bo cursed.

He wasn't a man who lied to himself, and he wondered why he'd started it now. If Mattie and he were alone, it would happen again, so that meant he had to work on the *alone* part. If this meeting didn't pan out, then he would see about placing her in someone else's protective custody.

Bo was thankful he'd already showered, and he went to the master bedroom and dressed as quickly as he could in his usual dark work pants and white button-up shirt. He clipped his badge to his belt.

Just as the doorbell rang.

Bo checked his watch. It was a little after 6:00 a.m., hardly the time for visitors. Hell. He hoped Ian hadn't returned. Just in case, he put on his shoulder holster and drew his gun. By the time he came out into the hall, Mattie was already there and looking very concerned. Unfortunately, that concern might be warranted now that the officers were no longer outside.

"Wait here," he instructed. Bo made his way to the front of the house, but instead of going to the door, he looked out the window of the dining room that was adjacent to the foyer.

He saw a delivery truck pulling away.

Then he spotted the package on the front step.

"Who is it?" Mattie asked.

Bo heard her footsteps and motioned for her to stay back. "A package."

"At this time of morning?"

But Bo didn't answer. He knew in his gut that there wasn't time. He turned, barreling toward Mattie, and he pushed her to the floor. It wasn't a second too soon.

The blast roared through the house.

Chapter Eight

Everything seemed to happen at once. Bo dove at her, tossing her to the floor. Mattie didn't have time to react or say anything.

And then there was the deafening sound.

Because she'd been on the run for so long, her first thought was that someone was trying to kill her. She fought to see what was going on, but Bo dragged her toward the laundry room.

Mattie soon saw why.

The front door had literally been blasted from its hinges, and there was smoke and debris whirling through the air.

My God.

She'd been right. Someone had tried to kill them.

Almost immediately, the alarm sounded from the security system. It was a piercing shrill that clamored through the entire house.

Bo pushed her into the laundry room, and he used the keypad on the wall next to the door that led to the garage so he could silence the alarms. Good. They needed to be able to hear what was going on.

He peered out into the hall, probably to make sure no one was coming through the gaping hole and into the house. He already had his gun drawn, but he took out his phone and called for assistance, both from the cops and the fire department.

"Who did this?" she asked the moment he hung up.

"I don't know, but I will find out."

It wasn't fear she heard in his voice but rather anger. No, not just anger. Rage. Because this attack had happened in his home, where just minutes earlier the babies had been. Mercy. They could have been hurt. Thank God Bo had insisted they go to the captain's house with the officers. They were safe.

She hoped.

"The children," she managed to say.

"The captain is there, and he'll make sure no one gets near them."

Mattie wanted desperately to believe that, but too many bad things had happened for her to be optimistic. Her purse with her gun was in the kitchen, and she wanted to run and grab it so she could hurry to the captain's house.

"We have to go," she insisted.

Bo shook his head. "It might not be safe to leave."

It hit her then. Yes, there had been damage to the door, only the door. There was no fire. No secondary explosion. No attack. And that meant this blast had gone off for only one reason: to get Bo and her running out of the house where an assassin could gun them down.

"But we can't stay here," she whispered, listening for any indication that they were about to be attacked.

"No. Not with that door wide open." He kept watch and reached behind him to take a set of keys from a hook on the wall. "As soon as a patrol car arrives, I'm getting you out of here."

Good. She didn't want to stay. Mattie wanted to go to the children.

The children, she mentally repeated.

Even though Jacob wasn't her child, Mattie felt a connection with the little boy, and she was just as worried about him as she was Holly.

The seconds crawled by, and they continued

to wait. It had probably been only a couple of minutes, but it felt like an eternity.

Mattie heard the autumn wind whistle through the opening created by the blast. She heard her own breathing. And Bo's.

But she also heard something else.

Something rattled.

It took her a moment to pick through the other sounds, and she realized it hadn't come from the front of the house but rather the back.

"Someone's trying to get in the back door, into the kitchen," Bo whispered.

That sent her stomach to her knees. God. When was this going to end?

Bo fired glances between the front and the back, and he kept his gun ready to respond in case there was another attack. Mattie could only stand there, listen and wait. She didn't have to wait long.

The doorknob rattled again, this time almost violently, and then there was the sound of wood being splintered.

Someone had kicked down the kitchen door.

And that someone was inside.

"I'm Lieutenant Duggan!" Bo called out. He pointed his gun to the ceiling and fired.

Even though it was clearly a warning shot,

the blast sent Mattie's heart pounding out of control. She needed her gun so she could try to defend them, but there was no chance she could go into the kitchen.

"Unlock the door," Bo told her, and he fired another warning shot into the ceiling. Bits of the acoustic tile rained down on them.

Mattie somehow managed to turn the latch, even though her hands were shaking. It obviously didn't help that she'd had experiences with nearly being killed, because the danger felt fresh and raw, just as the day when the gunmen had stormed the hospital.

"Get in the black SUV," Bo ordered, and he muscled her out of the laundry room and into the garage.

The large metal garage door was closed, thank goodness, so that gave them some protection in case there was someone at the front of the house waiting for them. But it would also trap them inside if an assassin came through the kitchen.

Mattie didn't waste any time. She got in the SUV, jumped into the passenger's seat and waited for Bo to follow her. But he didn't. He stayed in the doorway with his gun lifted high.

Had he seen the person who'd broken down the back door?

"Get in!" Mattie insisted. She didn't want him to stay put and be gunned down.

Mattie leaned over, threw open the driver's door and started the engine. Bo slammed the laundry room door and jumped into the SUV. In the same motion, he pressed the garage door opener clipped to his visor, and the large double door began to inch open.

"Put on your seat belt and stay down," Bo warned her.

Somehow Mattie managed to get the belt secured around her. Bo did the same. She slid as deep into the seat as she could but also kept watch of the laundry room door. It sickened her to think of an intruder inside Bo's home, but right now, she only wanted to get out of there.

The moment the garage door was fully open, Bo gunned the engine, and the SUV bolted down the driveway and into the street. She heard the sirens then. Thank God backup had arrived, because she wanted this would-be killer caught.

Mattie lifted her head just enough for her to check the rearview mirror, and she saw the laundry room door open. She caught just a glimpse of the man as he peered out but then quickly slammed the door shut.

She gasped.

"Yeah," Bo said. "I see him. It looks like Terrance Arturo, the guy from the van last night."

It did. But then she hadn't gotten more than a glimpse. If it was indeed Arturo, then that would lead them right back to Kendall. She didn't think it was a coincidence that Ian, Kendall's friend and employee, was also Arturo's attorney and that both had shown up at Bo's less than an hour after she'd arrived there.

While he sped away from the house, Bo took out his phone and pressed in some numbers. "O'Malley," he said a moment later. "No. We're all right. I have Mattie with me, and the twins were already at the captain's house, but I want additional officers dispatched there."

Her heart was practically pounding out of her chest, but that sped it up even more. Bo had assured her that the children would be safe, but if they needed extra officers, then he must believe they could be in danger.

"I just passed the officers responding to the scene," Bo continued, "but I want to get Mattie to headquarters before I come back and assist. Is Terrance Arturo out of jail?"

Mattie couldn't hear the officer's response, but Bo's profanity confirmed that the man was free. Free and responsible for an attack that could have killed them.

Well, maybe.

There had only been enough explosives to take out the front door, but a true killer would have put enough in that package to blow up the entire place. That meant this had probably been a kidnapping attempt.

And she had likely been the target.

"What?" Bo snapped, drawing her attention back to him. "He's there right now?"

Mercy, was he talking about Arturo? Or was there another attacker already at the captain's house? Mattie put her hand to her chest to steady her heart, and she waited and prayed.

"The children are fine," he said, obviously seeing her reaction. "But Terrance Arturo is out of jail, so he could have been responsible for that package."

Anger soon replaced the fear. "And we both know it was Kendall who was behind this."

Bo nodded, his expression as ripe with anger as hers. "We'll get a chance to ask him all about it. He's at headquarters with Ian Kaplan, and he wants to talk to you."

BO REMINDED HIMSELF that he was a peace officer. A twelve-year veteran of the SAPD and head of a large investigative unit. He couldn't just walk into an interview and beat someone senseless.

But that's exactly what he wanted to do to Kaplan and Collier.

Probably because of them, his home had been violated. Hell, *he* felt violated. And it would take a lifetime or two for him to come to terms with how close his children had come to being hurt. If they had been home and not at the captain's, then God knows what could have happened.

Plus, there was Mattie. Yet another attempt on her life, another nightmare to add to the memories of the ones already there. Mattie and he might be on different sides when it came to Holly, but she damn sure didn't deserve to bear this kind of burden all because she tried to do the right thing.

It was difficult, but Bo kept reminding himself of the *right thing* part. She wasn't responsible for any of this, and even though he hated that the danger had spilled over to his kids, he couldn't fault Mattie. No, the *fault* was inside the interview room waiting for a meeting they'd demanded.

"You're sure the children are all right?" Mattie asked again.

"I'm sure." He'd called both Rosalie and

the captain, and both had assured him that all was well.

It was *well* there at the captain's house, but Bo felt anything but well here at headquarters. He needed to get control of his temper before he walked into that room, because this might be the most critical interrogation of his life. Until he stopped the danger that centered around Mattie, his children might never be safe.

"Let me ask the questions," Bo insisted as they walked toward the interview room. He glanced at her. She was pale, and her lips were still trembling a little. "If you're not up to this, you can wait in my office."

She started shaking her head before he even finished. "No. I want to look Kendall in the eye. Ian, too. After what just happened, I want to strangle them both."

Bo felt the same way, and he hoped they both could hang on to their composure long enough to get some answers from these slimeballs.

Bo led Mattie not to the interview room but to the observation area next to it. Through the two-way mirror, they could see Ian Kaplan seated in the far right chair at the metal table. Next to him was a sandy-haired woman wearing a gray outfit.

"That's Cicely Carr," Mattie provided.

Kendall Collier's fiancée. "You said you know her?"

Mattie shrugged. "We grew up in the same social circles and went to the same private school. But I haven't spoken to her in years."

Social circles and private schools. Those were reminders that Mattie was wealthy and had probably had the best privileges that dirty money could buy. But she was anything but privileged now.

Cicely didn't exactly look the privileged part, either. Her clothes and hair were nice enough, but she certainly didn't scream "old money." She was somewhat of a plain Jane in her dove-gray suit that didn't seem to be tailored for her rail-thin body.

Bo followed Mattie's gaze, which was firmly on the man who was standing behind Kaplan and Carr.

Kendall Collier.

Bo recognized the man with the graying brown hair from the photos of his trial. Unlike his fiancée, Collier was dressed to perfection. He wore a midnight-blue suit that probably cost more than Bo made in six months. But while the suit screamed his social status, the man himself did not. Collier was pale, and even though he was standing, he was not moving, as if trying to conserve his energy. Bo had expected someone arrogant and impatient, but he didn't see any of that.

Bo led Mattie from the observation area and back into the hall. He paused, just long enough to allow her to change her mind, but she only opened the door and went inside.

"Mattie," Ian Kaplan and Cicely Carr said in unison. They got to their feet, and both were smiling.

"It's so good to see you." Cicely Carr came from around the table and wrapped her arms around Mattie.

Mattie went stiff and then eased herself out of the woman's grip. "Cicely, why are you here?"

"To help Kendall mend some fences with you." She looked at her fiancé and gave him a dazzling smile, which he didn't exactly return.

"I thought it would help if you talked to her," Kaplan added.

"The only one Mattie wants to talk to is me," Collier interrupted. He kept his distance on the other side of the table. "I'm here to bury the hatchet," he added, looking at Mattie.

"Bury it where—in my back?" Mattie snapped.

Carr shook her head. "It's not like that anymore. Kendall's a changed man—"

"Really?" Bo made the interruption this time. "Then who tried to kill Mattie this morning?"

Bo studied each of their reactions. Carr gasped and flattened her hand over her chest. Kaplan had just a flash of surprise—or else he faked it—but he resumed his poker face when he looked at Collier, whose reaction was the strangest of all. He seemed angry.

Seemed.

"Are you okay?" Kaplan asked Mattie. "Were you hurt?" He walked toward her, but Bo blocked his path.

"You think I'm responsible," Collier concluded. He groaned softly and scrubbed his hand over his forehead.

"Kendall didn't do this," Carr protested, turning toward Bo. "He's a changed man. I swear he is." She whipped back to Mattie. "Do you think we would be getting married if he hadn't changed?"

"People marry for all kinds of reasons," Mattie said, her eyes narrowing.

"Yes," Collier quietly said, and he repeated it. "I'm forty-nine, Mattie, and I want to be with my family. That's my priority now."

Carr slid her hand over her stomach. "Our

baby is due in seven months, and we want all of this bad blood to end before he or she comes into the world."

Mattie glanced down at Carr's stomach and then at Collier, who only nodded. Bo wasn't sure what to make of the moment. He'd interrogated enough people to know when someone was lying to him, but this didn't seem like a lie. Well, not about the baby, anyway.

"I've sold my business," Collier continued, looking at Bo now. "That'll be easy enough for you to check. There's nothing illegal going on. I've learned my lessons, and in part I can thank Mattie for that."

Mattie lifted her left eyebrow. "Is this for real?"

"Yes," Collier confirmed. Both Kaplan and Carr nodded in agreement.

"I feel as if I've stepped into an alternate universe," Mattie mumbled. Then she hiked up her chin and faced down Collier. "You had my fiancé gunned down."

"Not me." Collier pulled in a long breath. "But it was probably one of my former business associates. I believe they're the ones who tried to kill you immediately after the trial."

"Your business associates?" Mattie challenged, and her eyes narrowed again.

"I want names of these associates," Bo insisted.

Collier lifted his shoulder and slipped his hands into his pockets. "That wouldn't benefit anyone, especially Mattie, and it has cost me a great deal, but I've negotiated a truce with them. There will be no more threats on Mattie's life. She can find her child and bring him or her home."

"For the record," Kaplan added, "Kendall isn't admitting to any wrongdoing. He merely orchestrated a legal transaction that gave an amicable severance of ties to several of his former business associates."

Bo rolled his eyes at the legalese. "And I'm to take your word for this?"

"It's the truth," Carr insisted. She kept her attention fastened to Mattie. "We don't want any more problems, because we want to concentrate on our new life together."

"That's one of the reasons all three of us wanted to talk to you," Kaplan continued a moment later. "We want you to be able to get back to normal. And Kendall and Cicely want you back in the family." He paused a moment. "I'd especially like having you in my life again."

Bo didn't miss that last part. Mattie was right. This guy did have feelings for her, but Bo didn't know if they were real or of the sicko variety. Kaplan could be holding a grudge because Mattie had rejected him. That was often a motive for murder.

Collier's motive was obvious, too. Revenge for Mattie testifying against him. But Cicely Carr...well, she apparently loved Kendall Collier, and that made Bo wonder how far she would go to protect her baby's father. Was her adamancy about a new life just an act, or did her idea of a new life mean Mattie being out of the picture if she didn't cooperate with the game plan?

Mattie huffed and turned to Bo as if to ask what the devil was going on. He didn't know. But he would find out.

"Someone tried to kill Mattie just this morning," Bo reminded them. "If you worked out a so-called truce with your former business associates, then who was responsible for the attack?"

None of them jumped to answer that. Finally, Collier took a step forward. "I doubt you'd believe me."

"Try," Bo ordered.

"You should question Marshal Larry Tolivar."

Bo certainly hadn't expected that name to come up in this conversation. "Why?"

It was Kaplan who continued. "I've been trying to locate Mattie since she disappeared, and I've become suspicious of Marshal Tolivar. I think he's the one who allowed someone to hack into the Witness Protection database."

"You have proof?" Mattie asked.

"Not exactly, but if you dig into Tolivar's financials, you might find hints of a payoff. I believe someone, probably those former business associates, paid him and paid him well so they could access Mattie's files."

Bo didn't like the way Tolivar's name kept popping up. It was time to have the marshal investigated. "Your former business associates?" Bo questioned. "The ones that you won't identify because it'll get us killed?"

"Kendall would tell you if he could," Cicely Carr said as if it were gospel.

"I can't give you names," Collier reiterated. "But when you find the payoff that I believe Tolivar received, that should lead you to the people behind all of this."

He tipped his head toward the door. "Time to go."

"Not yet," Bo insisted. "Explain to me why you'd use a computer in a coffee shop to dig into my back-ground."

Kendall blinked, shook his head. "I have no idea what you're talking about."

"Really?" Bo pressed. "We have your prints."

"Then someone planted them there." He glanced at Mattie. "Someone's obviously trying to keep me in trouble with the law. And with you. Besides, why would I use a coffee shop computer? If I wanted to find out anything about you, I would have used one of my P.I.s. Or Ian."

True. Unless this really was some kind of intimidation tactic. Bo was either dealing with an innocent man or a very dangerous one.

"I've said my piece," Kendall Collier said a moment later. "And now Mattie needs some time to think."

Collier walked out first but not before he reached out to Mattie. She dodged his hand, stepping back. Her uncle nodded and seemed disappointed, but that was the only emotion he showed. Bo made another mental note: have Collier followed and see if SAPD could get authorization for some wire taps. If his shady business associates were responsible for what had happened, Bo wanted them identified and put behind bars, where they could never get to Mattie and the babies.

"Please give Kendall a chance," Cicely Carr whispered to Mattie. "Don't disappoint us."

That caused Mattie to pull her shoulders

back, and she was likely about to return fire over Carr's comment, but the woman walked out and hurried after Collier.

Ian Kaplan, however, stayed put. He took out his card and handed it to Mattie. "That's in case you've forgotten my number. We really need to talk. *Alone,*" he added, glancing at Bo.

"That's not going to happen," Mattie assured him.

Kaplan flinched as if she'd slapped him. "I'm trying to help you. That's why I pushed Kendall to put an end to all of this. I want you back in my life."

Well, there it was. All laid out. The lawyer still wanted Mattie. That riled Bo to the core. This moron could be responsible for the danger, and yet he was practically inviting Mattie to his bed.

Bo didn't want to think that what he was feeling was partly motivated by jealousy. But he couldn't totally dismiss that, either. Their kiss had changed things that shouldn't have been changed.

"I can help you find your child," Kaplan continued.

"How?" Bo snapped.

Kaplan shot him an irritated "get lost" look, but his expression softened when he turned his attention back to Mattie. "I can have an entire team of P.I.s out searching for the baby. All you have to do is say that you want my help."

And jump in his bed.

Bo felt his mouth bend into a snarl. "Specifics," he spelled out to Kaplan. "When you're ready to give specifics, Mattie and I will be ready to listen."

Kaplan's snarl matched Bo's. "Mattie and I can talk without you."

"No, we can't," Mattie spoke up. She huffed and pushed her hair away from her face. "Look, Ian, I'm not sure I even trust you, so we're not on the same side. And I'm not going to have any private conversations with you."

The color drained from the lawyer's face. "You're choosing Bo Duggan over me? Over your own family?"

"Bo protected me this morning. He put his life in danger for me. So, yes, I'm choosing him over you."

Kaplan sputtered out a few syllables before he finally seemed to regain his composure. "Call me when you change your mind." The man practically ran into Bo as he hurried out.

Mattie immediately leaned against the wall. Maybe it was the adrenaline catching up with her, or maybe this meeting had just drained her, but Bo held her because she looked ready to slide straight to the floor.

"I didn't expect this," she mumbled.

Neither had he. Bo slipped his arm around her waist and eased her to him. Her heart was pounding so hard, he could feel it against his chest.

"You think your uncle could be telling the truth about wanting a truce?" Bo asked.

"I don't know." She dropped her head onto his shoulder and gave a weary sigh. She leaned against him as if it were the most natural thing in the world.

It certainly felt natural, and that set off huge alarms in his head. He couldn't get this close to Mattie. But he didn't move, either.

"I just want the danger to be over," she whispered.

Bo was about to agree when he heard the footsteps. He pulled away from Mattie, but not before Captain Shaw Tolbert appeared in the doorway. His captain blinked and obviously noticed the close contact between Mattie and him.

"Rough meeting with her uncle," Bo managed to say, but explaining himself wasn't high on his priority list right now. "Who's with the children?"

"Several officers. Don't worry. They're safe."

"But for how long?" Mattie asked, her voice filled with emotion.

"For as long as it takes," the captain assured her. "I watched most of the meeting through the two-way. I already have someone working on a background check for the marshal, and I'll see what I can do about getting a search warrant so we can look through Kendall Collier's recent business records."

Good. The ball was already rolling.

"Cicely's family might be the business associates that Kendall was referring to," Mattie volunteered. "I don't have any proof, but her family is a lot like mine, and they've had dealings with Kendall in the past."

The captain and Bo exchanged glances. This hadn't come up in the original trial. They knew that Collier had received funding for the illegal arms deal, but the Justice Department had never been able to identify the source of that funding. Maybe it was Cicely Carr's family.

Or Carr herself.

"So what about their marriage?" Bo asked Mattie. "Is that legit?"

Mattie shrugged. "Could be. Even though Cicely is eighteen years younger than Kendall, she's always had a thing for him. Plus, I think her family always tried to push them together, but I had no idea that Kendall even thought of Cicely as a prospective partner. He usually goes for the flashier, more glamorous type."

Bo gave that some thought. "Maybe he's marrying her to appease her family and make peace with them."

"I'll look into that, too," the captain volunteered. He turned to Mattie. "Bo and I have to start making some security arrangements. A safe house for the twins," he clarified. "Why don't you wait in my office while we're doing that?"

She looked at Bo, and he nodded, only because the captain had *suggested* it. "Since you didn't get a chance to eat this morning, I'll have someone bring you some breakfast. And when the captain and I are done, I'll come and get you."

"My office is just up the hall." The captain pointed in that direction.

Mattie gave another hesitant glance before she walked away.

"Okay, what's wrong?" Bo immediately asked. "Did something happen to the twins?"

"No. Nothing like that." Captain Tolbert glanced out into the hall as if to make sure no one was listening. "I thought you might like to hear this without Mattie around."

A lot of bad things started to go through his mind. "What?"

The captain took out a piece of paper from his jacket pocket and handed it to Bo. "These are the results of the DNA tests we ran on Holly and Mattie."

Chapter Nine

Something was wrong. Mattie could feel it, and better yet, she could see it on Bo's face.

Bo was doing everything he should be doing—making the final arrangements for a safe house, checking on the investigation into Cicely's family and Marshal Larry Tolivar. He was even doing the paperwork about the explosion. From the moment he'd collected her from the captain's office and moved her to his, he'd been dealing with nonstop calls and questions.

What he hadn't done was look her in the eye.

And that meant something was wrong.

Mattie nibbled on the sandwich and chips that one of the uniformed officers had brought her, and she waited for an opening to question Bo about what had put him in such a mood. She even listened to the way he responded to the callers, but she couldn't hear anything specific that she didn't already know.

Was this about the kiss at his house and the embrace in the interrogation room?

Maybe.

Bo could be dealing with some guilt over what he was feeling for her and his loyalties to his late wife. Mattie was certainly dealing with some of that, too, but Brody had been dead nearly two years now. While a part of her would always love him, being on the run had taught her that life was too short to live in the past. She really wanted a chance at living in the present and planning a future.

"The safe house is nearly ready," Bo relayed to her when he finished his latest call. "It shouldn't be more than another hour at most. Setting up furniture and food for the twins is taking more time than we anticipated."

Of course. And that led her to something else that was on her mind. "Will I be at the safe house with all of you?"

There. She saw the flicker in his jaw. Something was definitely wrong, and that caused her heart to ache. Mercy, was he planning on sending her somewhere else just so she wouldn't be around Holly?

"You'll come with us," he mumbled and

continued to stare down at the paperwork he had positioned in front of him.

The relief was instant. "Thank you. I know that couldn't have been an easy decision for you to make, but I really appreciate—"

"The captain got the DNA test results back," Bo blurted out.

Mattie's pulse was suddenly thick and throbbing. She dropped the rest of the sandwich onto the wrapper and stood. Just getting to her feet was an effort. She felt as if all the bones in her body had crumbled on the spot.

Oh, God. This was why Bo had been dodging her gaze.

"And?" she prompted, though speaking was an effort, too. Everything inside was on hold, waiting.

"The test was a match." Bo looked at her now, and he stood, as well, facing her. "Holly is your biological child."

The breath whooshed out of her, and Mattie heard herself make some kind of sound. Part gasp, part sigh, but mostly it was a sound of relief. Even though she'd never doubted it, that precious little girl was hers.

When she started to laugh, she pressed her fingers to her mouth. She wanted to celebrate, jump for joy and shout it out so the world would know.

Holly was her baby.

But her joy went south when she saw Bo's expression. She'd never seen anyone in that much pain.

"I'm sure Nadine intended to tell you," Mattie said. But it was the wrong thing to say, because Bo only shook his head. Maybe there was no right thing to say in a situation like this.

Mattie walked closer to him, reached out and caught on to his hand. He pulled back, or rather tried to, but she held on. "I can't say I'm sorry about the test results. But I am sorry for what this is doing to you."

He glanced around as if he might tear out of the room. Or curse. Or yell. Or do a dozen other things to vent the emotion he was feeling. But he simply groaned and dropped back down into the chair.

"I didn't know," he mumbled. "I swear, I didn't suspect a thing until you showed up yesterday."

Mattie believed him. Nadine hadn't lived long enough to tell him the truth, and Mattie hadn't been in a position to try to claim her child.

She still wasn't.

"I can't just give her up," Bo insisted, his voice and face now tight with anger. "I can't just hand her over to you."

"I know." And it took every ounce of her courage to say that.

Bo blinked and stared up at her. "Then what the hell are we going to do?"

She gave his hand a gentle squeeze. "We're going to take the children to the safe house. We'll protect them, and when we know who's responsible for the danger, we'll work out what needs to be worked out."

That didn't appease him as she thought it would. He jerked away from her and cursed. "I'm the only father she's ever known. The only thing that needs to be worked out is for her to stay with me."

Mattie couldn't totally dismiss that. Bo had been part of her daughter's life since day one. "Holly loves you." She tried to keep her voice calm. Hard to do with the anger and emotion radiating from Bo. "I wouldn't dream of cutting you out of her life. I think we can work out visitation—"

"I don't want damn visitations!" he shouted. "I want my baby girl."

When he got up and bolted for the door, Mattie just grabbed him and held on. That put them body to body, of course, and they stood with her back against his closed office door and with Bo against her. The energy between them was so dangerous and strong that it frightened her.

But she wasn't scared of Bo.

Mattie was more frightened of her own reaction.

She had no intentions of giving up her child to this man, to anyone, but she couldn't deny this pull between them. It was too strong.

"Don't," Bo warned, but she had no idea what he was specifically warning her about.

Maybe she was giving off a signal of her intentions. And her intentions were apparently to kiss him, because that's what she did. Mattie came up on her toes and put her mouth to his.

Bo was stiff at first, and she thought he might pull away again. But he didn't. He ran his hand into her hair and jerked back her head so he could deepen the kiss. It was brutal and punishing, his mouth pressing hard and desperate while his body did the same to hers.

He didn't stop there.

He grabbed both her wrists in his other hand and pinned them against the door. He pinned her, too, giving her all his weight.

And all his anger.

While the kiss raged on, the middle of his body ground against hers. In the back of her mind, Mattie considered that she should be stopping this. Anger and kissing shouldn't be mixed, but with Bo, the mixture worked just fine. Yes, she was reeling from the news about her daughter. Yes, she was worried about the danger.

But she was also aroused beyond belief.

She wanted Bo, and she wanted him now.

Her body was on fire, and the kisses and body contact made her feel like a pressure cooker ready to go off. Until that moment, she hadn't been sure that Bo and she would become lovers, but she was certain of it now.

But *now* would have to wait.

She tore her mouth from his at the exact moment that someone knocked on his door. Bo stepped back, repeated some profanity and stared at her as if he couldn't believe what had just happened. Mattie was having trouble believing it, too, but she hoped it would happen again. And that made her very stupid. She shouldn't be playing around with Bo. No. He was too dangerous for that.

She moved to the side and tried to level her breathing before he threw open the door. It was the captain, and he gave them the same look as when he had caught them embracing in the interview room several hours earlier.

"I told Mattie," Bo admitted.

"And?" the captain asked when Bo didn't add anything else.

"We'll work it out." Bo seemed to issue that as some kind of challenge to her and to himself. "Are you here about the safe house?"

The captain shook his head. "I need you to come down to my office. Larry Tolivar just showed up, and he'd like to talk to both of you. Especially you," he said, looking at Mattie.

Well, Mattie wanted to talk to him, too. She wanted the truth about Kendall's accusation that the marshal had sold information about her in the Witness Protection Program.

"By the way, Tolivar already knows we're digging into his background," the captain explained. "And he's not very happy about it."

"He'll be even less happy about it when he talks to me." Bo started down the hall, and the captain and Mattie followed.

She considered asking the captain to postpone this little chat. After all, Bo was dealing with the fact that Holly wasn't his daughter. Hardly the time to be interrogating a suspect, but Mattie knew she stood no chance of stopping him. He needed somewhere to aim the emotions brewing inside him, and he might as well aim them at Tolivar.

The marshal was indeed in the captain's office, and he was pacing.

"Still alive, I see," Tolivar grumbled.

"Yes." She made sure her voice didn't waiver. Hard to do with everything she'd been through in the past twenty-four hours. "SAPD's taking good care of me."

Tolivar made a grunt of disagreement and aimed his glare at Bo. "You're having me investigated. Bad idea, Duggan. You don't want to play games with me."

"You're right. No games. I just want some answers. Did you send an explosive device to my house this morning?"

"I won't dignify that with an answer," Tolivar snarled.

"But you will," the captain insisted. "Answer Lieutenant Duggan's question."

That earned the captain a glare. "No. Of course not. I'm a peace officer, just like you, except I'm not some local yokel. I work for the federal government, and Mattie is in my protective custody."

"Not any longer," Bo said. "She left the program. I called your boss and let him know that about two hours ago."

Mattie hadn't heard him make that call, but

then he'd apparently made some before he moved her into his office. Good. She didn't want any association with Witness Protection or this man.

"Kendall Collier's hired someone to kill you," Tolivar insisted. "Investigating me or leaving protective custody isn't going to stop that."

"It might if we learn you have a connection to him," Mattie quickly pointed out. Suddenly all eyes were on her. "Kendall and perhaps someone close to him are the only ones who would have wanted to know my new identity and location. And you would have had access to it."

Tolivar aimed his index finger at her. "Someone hacked into the system. If you want to start assigning blame, then look to your uncle. He paid someone to do it, and it wasn't me."

"Then who?"

"Somebody close to Kendall Collier. Maybe his lawyer, Ian Kaplan, or maybe one of his hired henchmen."

"Funny," Bo remarked. "Kaplan said you were responsible for hacking into those files."

Tolivar flinched, obviously not expecting that. "Then he's lying through his teeth."

Bo shrugged. "Somebody is. That's why we're investigating anyone associated with this case. If you've got nothing to hide, then why don't you give us access to all your computer and financial records?"

The room got so quiet that you could have heard a pin drop.

"I don't share personal information with local cops," Tolivar finally barked. "And my advice is to back off, or I'll bring some heat down on SAPD."

The captain put his hands on his hips. "Is that a threat, Marshal?"

Maybe it was the steely look in the captain's and Bo's eyes, but Tolivar seemed to back down. "I just want to do my job and keep Mattie alive."

"She's no longer your job," Bo countered immediately. "In fact, you have no reason to be anywhere near her. Got that?"

The staring contest started, and Tolivar even took some steps so he'd be in Bo's face. "Yeah, I got that, Lieutenant. And when somebody blows her brains out, don't come crying to me."

With that, the marshal muscled his way past them and headed out.

"I want him followed," Bo said to the captain.

"Legally, we can't do that." The captain watched the marshal walk away. "But there's nothing that says I can't have an officer in Tolivar's general vicinity. I'll get someone on him." He took out his cell and made a call.

"Thanks." Bo put his hand on the small of Mattie's back and got her moving toward his office. They hadn't gotten halfway there when Bo's phone rang.

She held her breath, as she did with all the calls he received, but she always thought of the children. Of the danger. And Tolivar's visit had drilled home just how close that danger could possibly be.

"Everything's there?" Bo asked the caller. Whatever the answer was, it caused his forehead to bunch up. "Yeah. I'll tell her."

When Bo hung up, Mattie tried to brace herself for more bad news. "What now?"

It took him several moments to answer. "The safe house is ready. The twins… The children," he corrected, "are already en route." He motioned for her to follow him, and they reversed direction. "There's a car waiting to take us there so we can be with them."

It hit Mattie then as she was following Bo up the hall. This wasn't about the danger or the investigation. It wasn't even about the move to the safe house. It was about what would happen at the safe house.

"Yes," Bo said, as if he could read her mind.

Tear sprang to her eyes, because Mattie knew that soon, very soon, she would finally have her baby in her arms.

Chapter Ten

Bo felt sick to his stomach. Since Nadine's death, he'd worked so hard to give his children a normal, happy life. Hell, he'd worked to give himself that, as well.

Now everything was unraveling.

Mattie had DNA on her side. Ironic that a test he'd used to get convictions for killers and rapists was now a test that could cause him to lose his little girl.

He checked the rearview mirror again, something he'd done a lot on this half-hour drive. He had to make sure no one was following them, and that's the reason he'd driven all over the city. The safe house was only about ten minutes from police headquarters, but for safety reasons, he hadn't taken a direct route.

"It's going to rain," Mattie mumbled, looking out the car window and up at the sky.

Yeah, the clouds were heavy and gray, which suited his mood to a T.

"You think it'll storm?" she asked. Mattie had a firm grip on the remote control for the safe-house garage, and she'd had that grip on the small device since they'd picked it up earlier from police headquarters.

"I don't know." And he was more than a little surprised they were discussing the weather when they were just minutes from arriving at the safe house. Minutes away from Mattie taking the next step to claiming Holly. "Why?"

"I'm scared of storms," she answered.

He gave her a flat look. "You have a killer after you, Mattie. I think a storm is the least of your worries."

She nodded. Nodded again. And didn't say anything for several moments. "How are you handling this?"

Bo nearly laughed. "How do you think?"

Her gaze slid over him. "You look calm."

"Well, yeah. Looks can be deceiving. I've spent the last half hour trying to figure out how to stop this from happening." He paused. "I can't stop it, can I?" he added in a hoarse grumble.

"No." Now, she paused. "I wish Nadine had been able to tell you the truth that day.

Something more than 'Protect her.' There's no way you could have known what she meant by that."

Bo wasn't sure he wanted to open this can of worms, but he couldn't just let it go, either. "Did you know Nadine was dying when you left?"

"No. We were both weak from our deliveries, and we both kept nodding off. But when I left her, she was very much alive."

But already dying from the internal bleeding. Mattie couldn't have known about that. Nadine probably didn't, either. If she had, Nadine would have found a way to leave him a note or something.

"Nadine loved you very much," Mattie added.

Yes. He never doubted that. But that didn't make her death hurt any less. And now losing Holly was another cut, another wound that would never heal.

Bo pulled into the driveway of the safe house and took the remote from Mattie so he could open the garage door. There was another unmarked car with two officers parked just up the street, but now that he had arrived, they would probably leave. There wasn't enough manpower to devote three officers to protecting Mattie, but with the security measures

in the house itself and his own abilities, Bo
prayed he could keep everyone safe.

"It looks like a typical suburban house,"
Mattie remarked. She tapped her fingers on
the armrest, apparently impatient that it was
taking so long for the garage door to fully
open. "You're sure it's okay to be here right
in the heart of the city?"

"Hiding in plain sight is the best way." He
hoped. This particular place had a For Rent
sign out front, and SAPD had used it before
as a safe house for holding witnesses.

"Don't the neighbors suspect anything?"
Mattie wanted to know.

"No. We had a cop posing as a property
manager go around and tell everyone that this
place would be for short-term rentals." Still,
that didn't mean Bo wouldn't be on guard.
After all, the children were inside.

"Wait until the garage door closes before
you get out," Bo warned her. He pulled inside
the garage, turned off the engine and hit the
remote control again to shut the door.

Mattie looked as if she were preparing for
a sprint, and the moment the door closed, she
was out of the car. She raced to the entry,
but as Bo knew it would be, the door was
locked.

"Hurry," she insisted.

He unlocked the door and stepped back. Mattie ran inside. He followed her and hoped this wouldn't be traumatic for Holly. Bo already knew it would be traumatic for him.

Mattie hurried through the kitchen and into the living room. No kids. But he heard laughter coming from one of the bedrooms, and they headed in that direction. Rosalie was sitting on the floor playing building blocks with the kids. Thankfully, Mattie didn't go barging in. She held back, waiting, watching and crying.

Yeah, there were tears in her eyes.

Rosalie looked up, a smile on her face, but that smile faded when she spotted Mattie. "What's wrong?" she immediately wanted to know.

Even though Holly and Jacob were way too young to know what any of this meant, Bo didn't want to tell Rosalie in front of them. He motioned for the nanny to join him in the hall.

"Da Da!" Holly and Jacob called out in unison. Bo went into the room, scooped them up in his arms and gave them each a kiss. He kissed them like this every day, but today felt bittersweet.

Rosalie stood, hesitantly, and Bo put the babies back on the floor so he could step outside the room with Rosalie. Mattie stayed in the room and eased down on the floor, as well. She didn't get too close, but Jacob noticed his new *playmate*. He grabbed one of the plastic building blocks and brought it to her.

"Ta Ta," he said, meaning "thank you."

When Mattie smiled and repeated it, Jacob brought her even more of the blocks. Soon, Holly joined in on the game, but she wasn't nearly as adept at walking as Jacob. She wobbled and would have fallen if Mattie hadn't caught her in her arms.

The moment seemed to freeze.

Holly giggled and looked at Mattie. Bo could feel the love and emotion radiating from Mattie. This was the moment she'd no doubt dreamed about, a moment that had probably kept her alive and fighting.

The moment was a nightmare for Bo.

Holly had no idea that this woman was her biological mother, but she would soon grow to love Mattie. And that meant he would lose his baby girl.

"It's true?" Rosalie said softly. "She's really Holly's mother?"

"It's true," he managed to say.

"Tiss," Jacob announced when Mattie stacked some of the blocks. But he kissed

Holly's cheek first and then he kissed Mattie's. A moment later, Holly did the same.

When Holly's lips touched Mattie's cheek, Bo heard Mattie make a sound deep in her throat. It matched the love that was in her expression. And that's when he knew. Mattie wouldn't put up with this arrangement for long. She would no doubt demand custody as soon as she could.

Rosalie looked up at him. "What are you going to do?"

"I'll fight to keep Holly." But he didn't think it was a fight he'd win.

Still, he would fight. There was no other alternative. He couldn't just let Mattie rip Holly from his life, and even though she'd spoken of visiting rights and such, he didn't want that, either.

He wanted his daughter.

Bo wanted the life he'd had before Mattie had walked in and turned it upside down.

Mattie glanced back at him, as if to say she was sorry, but how could she be? She literally had everything she wanted in her arms.

"How long will we be here?" Rosalie asked.

Bo didn't take his eyes off Mattie and the children. "I'm not sure. Probably at least a day or two." He was being optimistic. The investigation was complex, with a lot of possibilities for things to go wrong.

Rosalie patted his arm in motherly fashion. "Find the person after Mattie," she reminded him. "And then you can get on to this business of the heart."

"Like I said, I'm not giving up Holly."

"I didn't mean that." Rosalie didn't continue until he looked at her. She touched her fingers to his chest. "I mean the matter of your heart."

Bo shook his head. "What are you talking about?"

Rosalie huffed. "It's as plain as the nose on your face that you're attracted to Mattie. She's attracted to you, too. It's also plain to see that you're both fighting it. My advice? Don't fight it anymore. Things might be easier to work out if you're loving and not snarling at each other."

Bo was sure he scowled. "Are you saying I should get involved with Mattie so I can keep Holly?"

"No. I'm saying you should get involved with Mattie because you want her. The custody issue would just be an added benefit."

He didn't curse because he wasn't sure he could keep the kids from hearing.

"Just think about it," Rosalie added and headed for the kitchen.

She left Bo there to stew. Yes, he was attracted to Mattie. Hell, he got aroused just thinking about her, and he kept getting a very vivid image of her naked and in his bed. Her legs wrapped around him while he buried himself deep inside her.

But that wasn't going to happen.

Was it?

That question hit him damn hard.

If they kissed again, it just might happen whether he intended it to or not. Wanting Mattie overrode his common sense, and that meant he needed to solve this case so he could concentrate, as Rosalie had put it, on matters of the heart.

He stepped farther back into the hall and took out his phone so he could call Sergeant O'Malley for an update. Mattie glanced back again, probably when she realized he was calling someone. Her left eyebrow lifted to ask if everything was okay. Bo just nodded. She nodded back and gave him a brief smile.

And Bo wondered when the hell things had gotten so easy between them that they could communicate without words.

"O'Malley," Bo greeted when the sergeant

answered. "Tell me you have some good news. Any good news will do."

"Well, it's news all right. I'll let you decide whether it's good or not. We have our techs digging through the financials for Cicely Carr's family. If they were involved in the illegal arms deal with Kendall Collier, then it's not there in the records. Carr, however, is a different matter."

"What do you mean?" Bo was definitely interested in the information, but he also didn't take his attention off Mattie, whom Jacob had coaxed into stacking blocks with Holly and him.

"She withdrew a good portion of her trust fund about the same time the illegal arms deal took place, and we can't find where that money went."

"Why didn't this come up during the FBI investigation?" Bo asked.

"Because she hid the deal through several layers of corporate red tape. Besides, the FBI was focusing on her parents, not her."

So, Cicely Carr could have given or loaned money to Kendall Collier. Was that now the reason Collier was marrying her? To keep her quiet?

"There's more," O'Malley continued. "This is the part that might be good or bad. I'm looking at the whole arms deal with a fresh eye, and Collier might have been telling the truth about his involvement. He honestly might not have known he was investing in illegal weapons. Before this incident, he'd done business with the dealer, Armand Brier, and it appears that Brier bundled the arms deal along with other investments."

"Then why did the FBI pursue Collier?" Bo asked.

"Because he did try to cover it up after he learned about it. That's about the time Mattie came into the picture. She found the documents, heard some of Collier's phone conversations and maybe thought he'd honchoed the deal."

Hell. So maybe Mattie had gotten herself in scalding hot water by testifying against a man who wasn't the primary player. "But someone killed Mattie's fiancé and tried to kill her," Bo pointed out.

Bo checked to make sure Mattie hadn't heard that, but her attention stayed firmly on the kids.

"Yeah," O'Malley agreed. "My theory is that the initial attacks were orchestrated by this Armand Brier. He probably wanted to do away with Mattie or anyone else who could have sent him to prison for the arms deal."

"Then, why didn't Brier go after Collier?" Bo wanted to know.

"I'm not sure. Maybe they came up with some sort of compromise. After all, Collier would have gone to prison, too, because he did cover up the deal after the fact."

Yes, but that wasn't nearly as bad as what Brier had done. Of course, Bo wasn't about to cut Collier any slack. "So you think Brier sent that explosive to my house?"

"No," O'Malley quickly answered. "Brier was found dead about four months ago. He was shot and killed near his office in London. An apparent robbery gone bad."

Or else Collier had eliminated the one man who could send him to jail. Now he might be out to eliminate Mattie just so he would have the assurance and maybe a little revenge.

"Thanks for all of this," Bo told O'Malley. "I'll talk to Mattie about Cicely Carr and see if she knows anything that can help with the investigation. And I'll tell her about Brier's death, of course."

"There's more," O'Malley said before Bo could hang up. "We followed Tolivar as the captain requested, and we saw something odd. He's meeting with Ian Kaplan right now, as we speak."

"Kaplan?" Bo said that loud enough that it

caused Mattie to look at him. He held up his finger in a "wait a second" gesture to let her know he'd fill her in. "Let me guess. Tolivar is ready to beat Kaplan to a pulp because Kaplan told us that Tolivar is the one who's after Mattie."

"Not exactly. I don't know what's going on, but this meeting isn't what we expected."

Confused, Bo shook his head. "What do you mean?"

"I'm sending a picture to your cell," the sergeant explained. "In this case, a picture's worth a thousand words."

Bo pressed the button to open the image, and he watched as it loaded on to the tiny screen. Bit by bit, the image became clearer.

"Hell," Bo mumbled.

What was going on?

Chapter Eleven

Mattie was not a happy camper.

Here she should be spending the rest of the day with her daughter, but instead she was at police headquarters again. She could blame Larry Tolivar for that.

And Ian.

She studied the photo on Bo's phone. A photo of Tolivar and Ian, two men who were supposedly ready to throw each other under a bus with one accusing the other of wanting her harmed. Yet that wasn't the case in the photo. They were shaking hands and smiling as if a friendly meeting were normal for them.

Maybe it was.

"I've known Ian for years," Mattie told Bo as they walked toward the interview room where Ian was waiting for them. She handed Bo his phone. "But until I went into Witness Protection, I'd never seen Tolivar. Never heard Ian mention him, either."

"Well, they're pretty chummy in that picture," Bo snarled.

Yes, they were. And that's the reason Bo had called Ian the moment he'd seen it and demanded that he come to headquarters to answer some questions. Bo had called Tolivar, as well, but the marshal hadn't answered his phone. So that meant Ian would be providing any initial information about the encounter.

In other words, this might be a total waste of time.

Still, Bo had to investigate the meeting between the two suspects, and even though Bo had insisted that she could stay at the safe house, Mattie had decided to come anyway. The sooner she got to the bottom of what was happening to her, the sooner she could get on with her life.

And her life was with Holly.

Soon, very soon, she'd have to figure out how Bo fit into the picture. Or if he fit in at all. He was still reeling from the news of the DNA test, but he also might be gearing up to battle her in court. They might find themselves enemies if they weren't already. Too bad this was one enemy that she wanted in an entirely different way.

Mattie wanted more of those hot, out-of-control kisses. She wanted Bo to take her

just as those kisses had suggested he might.
Hard and fast, where she didn't have to think
about the consequences. She'd spent too many
months planning and plotting. Running and
hiding. And now what she wanted was to
spend time with her daughter.

And have sex with Bo.

She felt her face flush. Felt her body go
warm in anticipation of what parts of her were
suggesting. Of course, her brain was telling
her to back off, and she probably would. But
she was secretly hoping Bo would take this
to the max.

"You okay?" Bo asked, stopping outside
the interview room door. "You're flushed, and
you're breathing funny."

"Oh." She quickly tried to fix that. Talk
about wearing her heart on her sleeve.

"Oh?" Bo questioned.

Since she didn't want to verbalize anything
right now, she didn't answer. She just stared
back.

"Oh," Bo finally said, and he huffed. "Yeah.
We'll deal with that later."

"How?" she blurted out. Great. Now, she'd
just opened a box that should be left closed.

The corner of his mouth lifted and he
crushed his mouth against hers for just a split

second. "How the hell do you think we'll deal with it?"

No smile this time. He glanced around as if to make sure no one was around to hear what he was about to say. "Just in case you overheard Rosalie and me talking earlier, I want you to know that how we deal with this heat has nothing to do with how we deal with Holly."

"Why would it?"

"Exactly." He made a grunt of agreement. "Rosalie thinks we'll be more amicable to each other if I'm…well…having sex with you." It sounded as if those weren't the words he wanted to use. He likely had something much more crude on the tip of his tongue.

"Amicable," she repeated. Mattie blushed. That wasn't the word she would use, either. "It would be very…" And here she tried to figure out the best way to put it. "Satisfying."

"Hell," he mumbled and then added something much harsher. "When and if I get you in my bed, I won't be aiming for something just satisfying and amicable. I figure if we're going to screw up our lives, then it might as well be something to remember."

All right. That stole her breath away as only Bo could do. He gave her another of those crushing kisses on the mouth that in no way qualified as a peck, then threw open the door to the interview room.

Ian smiled when he spotted her, but that smile evaporated when his attention landed on Bo. Or maybe what caused his smile to fade was that he might have sensed the sexual energy between Bo and her. Mattie was certain they looked guilty of something.

"I didn't know if you'd come," Ian told her.

"I wasn't sure I would, either." She tipped her head to the photo on Bo's phone. "But I really wanted an explanation for that."

When Ian looked at the picture, his face dropped, and he gave a weary sigh. "You have this all wrong," he insisted, thrusting the phone back in Bo's hand.

"Really?" Bo challenged. "Why don't you tell me just how wrong I have it, because you see, you and the marshal look like old friends."

"We're not," Ian snapped, and he repeated it when he shifted his attention back to Mattie. He stared at her a moment and scrubbed his hand over his face. "Look, I decided to play nice with Tolivar because I want you to be safe. I don't want you hiding out with the cops. Especially this cop," he added, tossing a glare at Bo.

Bo stepped closer, violating Ian's personal space. "So what did you learn from playing nice?"

Ian's glare softened, and he sighed again. "Nothing that I didn't already know, but I think Tolivar is willing to keep talking to me. He thinks I'm just Kendall's flunky, so maybe he'll let something slip when he's spouting off how much he wants to take Mattie back into custody. I want him to admit that he planted Kendall's fingerprints on that coffee shop computer. I want him to give me any information that'll help me put him behind bars."

"You really think Tolivar is dirty?" Bo pressed.

"You bet I do. It makes sense, too. He would have had the expertise to plant Kendall's fingerprints. He could have sold the info in the Witness Protection files and made it look like a hack job."

"Of course, that brings us right back to Kendall. Or you," Bo added. "You two are the ones who wanted to find Mattie and had the strongest motive for paying someone to give you her whereabouts."

"I won't deny that," Ian admitted.

Bo paused, obviously waiting for more, but it didn't come. "Are you admitting you paid

Tolivar to hack into the Witness Protection database?"

"You know I can't admit to that." He looked at Mattie when he spoke. "That would be a felony. But I will say I was desperate to find you, and I knew you'd want to be reunited with your daughter."

It was as if all the air went out of the room. Mattie sucked in her breath. "You knew I had a daughter," she accused. "And you knew where she was."

Ian stepped around Bo and reached out to put his hand over her shoulder, but Mattie moved away before that could happen. Ian glanced away, mumbled something and then finally nodded. "Yes."

"How did you find out?" Mattie demanded.

"By having some of my P.I.s follow Larry Tolivar. He's like a pit bull. He just wouldn't let go of it, so I had him followed. One of my P.I.s spotted him breaking into Lieutenant Duggan's SUV, so I figured this might be connected to him."

"Wait," Bo said when Ian was about to continue. "Your man saw the marshal break into my SUV and you didn't report it?"

"No reason. The guy didn't take anything. He just swabbed the infant car seats and taped them down for hair samples."

There was only one reason Mattie could think of that someone would want to do that—to get a DNA sample. She wasn't sure the Justice Department had her DNA on file, but she was betting they did.

"After the marshal went to Duggan's house, I put one and one together," Ian explained. "After all, the lieutenant has two babies who are the exact age that your child would be."

Mattie looked at Bo to see if he was buying this. Maybe. Ian was making a good argument.

"You're positive you didn't know about my baby until yesterday?" she asked.

Ian looked her straight in the eyes. "I swear. Mattie, if I had known where your baby was, I would have tried to get her for you."

Bo cursed, and Mattie touched him to stop him from grabbing Ian and putting him up against the wall. She couldn't stomach the thought of Ian trying to take Holly. Bo was obviously having trouble with that, as well.

"You would have tried to get her," Mattie repeated. "Ian, I don't want you involved in this. And I especially don't want you trying to take my child."

He tried to touch her again, but this time Bo batted the man's hand out of the way, using far more force than necessary.

"Am I interrupting anything?" someone asked. The door was ajar, and someone pushed it fully open. It was Cicely Carr. "I asked at your office," she said to Bo. "And they told me you were here."

Cicely volleyed glances at all of them, and her forehead bunched up. However, Mattie figured she'd heard at least the last part of the conversation and knew what had prompted the uncomfortable silence.

"Why are you here?" Cicely asked Ian. She didn't seem pleased that her fiancé's attorney was at the police station again.

"Mattie and I had some things to clear up," Ian snarled. He grabbed his briefcase from the table. "But it's useless. She doesn't trust us, Cicely. She only trusts this cop here."

Cicely smiled, and Mattie wondered if anyone could be that sappy sweet and still be genuine. "Of course she trusts us. We're practically family. Mattie just needs some time, right?"

Mattie huffed. "What I need is proof of who's trying to kill me."

"Well, you can cross Kendall and me off that list. And Ian," the woman added after a long pause. "That's why I wanted to see you again. To tell you that all of this digging into my family's records isn't necessary. I'll tell you anything you want to know, because Kendall and I have nothing to hide."

Bo took the woman up on that offer. "Did you give Kendall the money for his part in the illegal arms deal?"

"Cicely," Ian said as a warning. "You don't have to answer that."

"But I will. If it'll make Mattie realize we're on her side now." Cicely squared her shoulders and turned to Bo. "Yes, I gave Kendall the money, but neither of us had any idea it was for illegal arms. And no, my parents weren't involved. I gave Kendall money from my trust fund. So there, you can stop digging and stop asking questions. We're all on the same side now."

"So you keep saying," Mattie mumbled. "But the bottom line is someone killed Brody." Her voice cracked a little when she said her late fiancé's name. "Someone tried to kill Bo and me just this morning."

Cicely gave a long sigh and kept her gaze on Mattie. "What will it take to convince you that Kendall wasn't behind any of that?"

"What will convince me? Finding proof that someone else did it."

Cicely paused a moment and then gave a crisp nod. "All right. Let me see what I can find out."

"Don't," Bo warned. "If you're truly innocent in this, then your questions could get you killed. Someone wants to silence Mattie permanently, and this person might not like you trying to finger him."

Cicely paused again. "That's a chance I have to take. For Kendall. He wants Mattie back in his life. Other than me and our unborn child, she's the only family he has left. Family's important to him now."

Mattie folded her arms over her chest. "Why now? Kendall's never shown once ounce of family concern for me. What happened to make him change?"

"I happened," Cicely said, hiking up her chin. "Kendall fell in love with me, and love changed him. Love, and our baby." She slid her hand over her stomach.

Ian cleared his throat, drawing everyone's attention back to him. The attorney just stared at Cicely. "You might as well tell them the rest."

"The rest?" Bo demanded when Cicely didn't answer.

"Kendall is dying," Ian announced.

Well, Mattie hadn't seen that bombshell coming. Apparently neither had Bo, because he looked surprised, suspicious even, but not especially concerned.

"Kendall's not dying," Cicely corrected. "But he does have aplastic anemia. It's a blood disorder where the body doesn't make enough red blood cells. He's on medication, and we're searching for a bone marrow donor. Once he has the bone marrow transplant, he'll be fine."

"But so far, there's been no donor match," Ian explained.

"Is that what this is all about?" Mattie snapped. "Kendall wants me to be a donor?"

"You're not a match." Ian, again. Cicely was just standing there sniffing back tears. "You were already in the National Bone Marrow Registry, so we checked."

That was true. She'd become a registered donor years ago when a friend had needed a marrow transplant.

Mattie got a really bad feeling about this. "But my child could be a match."

Cicely didn't say anything. She just kept sniffling. However, Ian finally nodded.

Mattie cursed, and she turned so quickly that Bo had to catch her or she would have fallen.

"Get out of here," Mattie demanded.

"We don't want to hurt the child," Cicely insisted. "We just want her tested to see if she's a match."

"And you thought the best way to do that was to kill or kidnap me?"

"We didn't do those things," Cicely practically yelled. "We only want the baby."

"Well, you're not going to get her." Bo kept his voice calm, though Mattie didn't know how he managed it. Since he already had hold of her, he got her out of the room.

"You can't let Kendall die!" Cicely shouted. "I love him, and I won't let you do this to him."

Mattie ignored Cicely's ranting, but she heard every word. And every word was motive for why someone had tried to blow up Bo's home. That perhaps hadn't been a murder attempt but a kidnapping. If Cicely or Kendall had her, then that would get them one step closer to her baby and the bone marrow that Kendall apparently needed to live.

"We need to get back to Holly," Mattie mumbled.

Bo obviously understood that, and that's why he was hurrying down the hall with her. "We need to be careful, though. They could have told us about the bone marrow so that we'd rush back to the safe house. I can't do that. I have to make sure they aren't following us."

"Of course. I wouldn't put it past them."

He led her out of the building, but he didn't go to the unmarked car that he'd left in the parking lot. "We have to switch cars," he let her know. "If Cicely Carr or Kaplan had someone watching the parking lot, they could have seen us drive up, and then they could have planted a tracking device on the vehicle. It wouldn't have been easy to do, but it might have worked if their hired help was wearing a fake cop's uniform."

That caused her breath to race. "And a tracking device would have led them straight to Holly."

"That's not going to happen." He took her to the motor pool garage and checked out another vehicle.

"Do you think your uncle's in love with Cicely?" Bo asked as they got in the new vehicle.

"I doubt it." She lifted her shoulder. "I could be wrong, though."

"And she could have gotten pregnant to give him a chance at getting another bone marrow donor."

She nodded. "True. Plus, there's the fact that they can't be forced to testify against each other if they're married."

And it would probably work. Of course, if there was no new evidence against Kendall, there likely wouldn't be another trial anyway, especially with the arms dealer already dead.

Mattie didn't say a word until they were out of the parking lot and on their way. "Maybe this means Kendall no longer wants me dead."

"Maybe."

He kept watch in the side and rearview mirrors. So did Mattie. No one pulled out of the parking lot with them, but there were plenty of people in the area. Some in parked cars on the streets. Some milling around. One of them could have been hired to watch for them.

"Maybe?" she questioned.

He hesitated a moment. "If you're dead, then as your next of kin, Kendall could petition to get custody of Holly."

"Oh, God." She rammed her fingers through her hair and repeated it. "I have to draw up a will naming you as her guardian. And I have to let Kendall know that killing me won't get him Holly."

"You could also let him think you'll cooperate with the bone marrow test."

Her gaze flew to his. "What do you mean?"

"If you tell Kendall that you'll have Holly tested, then that buys us some time. We're close to figuring all of this out, Mattie, and we just need to give Kendall a little something so that he backs off."

She gave that some thought. "But what if it's not Kendall who's after me? What if it's really Marshal Tolivar?"

Then he and Mattie could have even bigger problems. Tolivar could come after Mattie, maybe to silence her, maybe to kill her, and Kendall and his cronies could try to take Holly.

"Oh, God," Mattie mumbled again.

Obviously, Bo knew what they were up against. And right now, Mattie just wanted to get back to the safe house so they could protect Holly.

Mattie huffed when they caught the red light just one block up from headquarters, and she checked around them again. Nothing seemed suspicious or worth mentioning to Bo.

"If I let Kendall think I'm going to cooperate and have Holly tested, what next?" Mattie asked. "Do I actually go through with the test?"

Bo didn't answer. Mattie followed his gaze and saw that Bo had zoomed in on a man who was about twenty feet away and walking toward them. The guy was wearing a baseball cap slung low over his face and a raincoat. While there was indeed rain in the forecast, the garment, and the man, gave Mattie an uneasy feeling.

"You think he could be a problem?" Mattie asked, just as the light turned green.

Mattie held her breath, waiting for the car in front of them to move. But that didn't happen. The vehicle still didn't budge when the cars behind them started to honk their horns.

That's when Mattie knew they were in trouble.

Bo grabbed Mattie and pushed her lower into the seat. Good thing, too. Because the man whipped out a gun from beneath his raincoat.

And he fired right at them.

Chapter Twelve

Mattie heard the blast. Thick and loud, it echoed through the busy street. Despite the fact that it sounded exactly like a car backfiring, she knew that wasn't the case.

The sound was a gunshot.

"Stay down!" Bo shouted, drawing his gun from his shoulder holster.

Mattie wanted to remind him to stay down, as well, but the next shot drowned out her voice. The windshield shattered, cracking and webbing, except for the gaping hole in the center.

A hole caused by a bullet.

That put her heart in her throat. Mercy, they were literally out in the open and right in the shooter's line of fire. The next bullet proved that. It ripped through what was left of the windshield and dropped a chunk of safety glass right onto her.

Bo tossed her his phone. "Press the first number and tell them we need help."

Mattie had no idea how she managed to press the button to make the call. Her hands were shaking violently.

"O'Malley," the officer answered.

"Someone's shooting at us." She looked up at the street signs. "We're on St. Mary's." Though she couldn't see the cross street.

"I'm on the way," O'Malley assured.

"Get down!" Bo called out, and it took her a moment to realize he wasn't talking to her but to the half dozen or so pedestrians on the sidewalk. Most were already ducking for cover or running.

All except the tall man wearing a raincoat. Although she couldn't see his face, something about him was familiar.

"I can't return fire," Bo said. With his gun still at the ready, he ducked down. "Too many people."

That didn't stop the gunman, though. He fired another shot into the car, and Mattie heard it slice through the door right next to her.

Bo cursed and jammed his foot onto the accelerator, plowing their vehicle right into the car ahead of them. There was no driver inside. Maybe he'd run the moment the bullets started firing as the other drivers had done. Or maybe it was more sinister than that. This guy could have been in on this attack. Either way, since there were vehicles on three sides and the gunman on the remaining side, it meant they were trapped.

An image of Holly flashed through Mattie's mind. Mattie and her baby might never get to know each other, and that broke her heart. But what broke it even more was that both Jacob and Holly could become orphans if Bo and she couldn't get out of there.

She cursed because she didn't have her gun with her. She could grab Bo and try to run for cover, but the gunman was better positioned. Even though the car wasn't much protection, it was better than being out in the open where they could be gunned down.

"Enough of this," Bo mumbled, and he took aim and fired. Not at the man but into the air so that it wouldn't hit any innocent bystanders.

Through the side window, Mattie saw the gunman dive to the sidewalk, joining the others already there.

She wanted to cheer. The danger wasn't over, not by a long shot, but at least Bo's shot had caused the gunman to stop shooting. Mattie doubted the lull would last long.

Bo didn't waste any time. He gunned the engine again, his front bumper grinding against the much larger car in front of them. Finally, it moved, but not enough to give Bo room to maneuver them out of there.

Mattie kept her attention focused on the gunman, and she nearly screamed when she saw him lift his head from the sidewalk.

And his gun.

"He's going to shoot again," she tried to warn Bo. But it was too late.

The gunman fired. The bullet slammed through the car and right into the seat, less than an inch from her arm. The next one went into her headrest.

Well, it was clear which one of them the gunman wanted dead. This attack was for her, but the gunman probably didn't care if he killed Bo in the process.

Bo cursed and hit the accelerator again, ramming into the other car. It worked. The jolt sent the car forward and finally gave Bo the opening he needed. He jerked the steering wheel to the left. With the tires squealing and the bullets continuing to blast through their car, Bo got them away from there.

"O'Malley's on the way," Mattie relayed to him. She tried to brace herself for more of the shots, for the deafening deadly blasts.

But they stopped.

Bo grabbed his phone and made another call. Unlike her, he was able to give a more specific address and a description of the gunman. He also requested an ambulance in case any of the bystanders had been hit.

Mattie didn't sit up, but she lifted her head just enough that she could see the side mirror. And what she saw had her just as frightened as the prospect of more bullets coming their way.

"The gunman's running," she practically shouted.

She didn't want him to escape. Mattie wanted the cops to arrive right now and arrest him. Then they could force the man to tell them who'd hired him. That information was critical, and once they had it, then this danger might finally end.

"Don't let him get away," Bo told the officer on the other end of the line. He continued to maneuver the car through the busy streets, quickly putting some distance between them and the gunman.

"He wanted me dead," Mattie mumbled.

"Yeah." Bo reached up and tore away what was left of the safety glass. "But we're going to get him."

She latched on to that promise and continued to watch. And pray. Mattie hoped he didn't have some way of following them and launching another attack.

Or…

"We need to get to the children now," Mattie blurted out. She suddenly had an overwhelming need to make sure that that wasn't where the gunman was headed next.

"We can't go to them. Not now."

Mattie frantically shook her head, ready to argue with him. She had to make sure the children were okay.

"This could have all been a ruse," Bo explained. "While we were pinned down, someone could have put a tracking device on the car."

"I didn't see anyone do that." But she couldn't say with 100-percent certainty that it hadn't happened.

"There was a lot going on," he went on while he maneuvered the car through the side streets. "And it's too big of a risk to take. We can't compromise the location of the safe house. Plus, we can't drive into the neighborhood with the car shot up like this. It would draw attention to us, and we don't need that."

Mattie knew this was all true, but each moment she was away from the kids was agony. It obviously was for Bo, as well, because he took out his phone again and made another call. This one he put on speaker.

"Rosalie," he said the moment the nanny answered. "Is everything okay?"

"Yes, but I was about to ask you the same thing. The officer here with us just got a call that something had happened to Mattie and you?"

"It was probably a case of wrong place, wrong time," Bo lied. "But we're all right."

Another lie. Mattie was shaking and wasn't sure she could stop. But she was also relieved. Rosalie and the children were safe.

For now.

She wanted to tell Bo to have another officer sent out, but that might not be smart, either. Heck, the person after them could be watching headquarters for just that sort of thing. Bo was right. Best to return to the station and regroup. And get another car.

"I'll phone you from headquarters," Bo assured Rosalie. "I'll also be tapping into the security feed at the house…because I want to take a look at the babies. I think Mattie would like that, too."

Yes. She would. Right now, just seeing them would help soothe her.

"Do you see anyone following us?" he asked Mattie right after he ended the call.

"No. But with all the traffic, it's hard to tell." Then what Bo did really sunk in. "You don't think the gunman will follow us to police headquarters and start shooting at us there?"

He didn't answer her right away. "We'll be careful when we get out at the parking lot."

Oh, God. This might not be over.

It seemed to take a lifetime, but they finally reached the headquarters building. Bo parked the bullet-riddled car next to the side entrance, and true to his word, he hurried them inside.

No one fired shots at them.

Several officers asked how they were, and Bo gave them a clipped answer that they were unharmed. He didn't stop, however. He got them to his office, and while he rang Rosalie he used the laptop on his desk to tap into the safe house security system. Mattie soon saw the children sleeping in their cribs.

"What happened?" Rosalie whispered, and she went into the hall, probably so she wouldn't wake the children. Since Bo had the call on speaker, Mattie had no trouble hearing the woman.

"Someone fired a few shots at us after we left headquarters."

Because she was still in camera range, Mattie saw the stark fear on the woman's face.

"But it's all right," Bo assured her. "As soon as we can, Mattie and I will be back. In the meantime, just stay inside and keep everything locked up. The officer is still there with you, right?"

"In the living room. He hasn't left the house."

"Good. Make sure it stays that way." There was a tiny beep from his phone. "Rosalie, I have another call coming in, but I'm going to keep the security feed on for several more minutes."

So he could keep watch. Mattie was thankful for it. Just seeing both children, safe and sleeping, made her breathe easier.

"O'Malley," Bo said when he took the other call. "What's going on?"

"We're in pursuit, but we have an ID. One of the officers recognized him. It's Terrance Arturo. Gotta go. I'll call when we have him."

Terrance Arturo. That turned her blood to ice. "Didn't they arrest him?" she asked.

Bo nodded. "But they had to release him."

Mattie squeezed her eyes shut a moment. "Arturo works for Ian and therefore Kendall."

Bo nodded again, and he slipped his arm around her waist. "When he's caught, I'll question him. If Ian or Kendall ordered this hit, then I'll get the truth from Arturo." Bo eased her closer to him. "You should sit down. You're shaking."

Yes, she was, and since Mattie wasn't sure she could stand much longer anyway, she slid to the floor, using the wall to support her back. Bo took the laptop and slid down right next to her, but they were only there a few seconds when Mattie heard something on the security feed from the safe house. It was Jacob. He'd woken up and was starting to fuss.

Rosalie immediately went to the little boy, picked him up and started to rock him. Bo zoomed in on that tiny precious face, and it brought home exactly what was at stake here.

Their children.

"If Arturo isn't caught," Mattie whispered, "I'll call Kendall and start the process to make him think that I'll help him, that I'll have Holly tested as a possible bone marrow donor."

Bo didn't say anything, but that got his jaw

muscles working. It was a decent backup plan, but he obviously hated the idea as much as she did. She didn't want Kendall even speaking her daughter's name until she was sure he wasn't the one trying to kill her.

Jacob lifted his head from Rosalie's shoulder and looked directly into the camera.

"Hey, grumpy," Bo teased his son. Bo touched his fingers to the screen.

"He can hear you?" Mattie asked.

"No. The audio feed is one-way. We can only hear them. It's for security reasons so that if someone manages to get access to the security system, they won't be able to backdoor their way into the police computer."

That made sense, but she would have liked the little boy to hear their voices.

"He looks so much like you." She studied the tiny face still staring at them as if he knew they were on the other end of that camera. "I didn't see it so much when he was born, because I didn't know what you looked like then, but I see it now."

"You held him when he was born?" Bo asked.

"Yes. I guess you could say I delivered him. I cut the cord with a pair of scissors I found in the nurses' lounge. Nadine had done the same for me about a half hour earlier when Holly was born." Mattie lifted her shoulder. "Maybe that's why I feel so close to Jacob, because I was there with him right from the start."

The pain and tension returned to Bo's face, and she was sorry she'd brought it up. He took a deep breath, kissed the top of her head and then slipped his left arm around her so he could pull her to him. Until they pressed together.

Like a real couple watching their family.

Mattie stiffened at that thought and cursed herself for even thinking it. It didn't matter how many kisses they'd shared. It didn't matter how hot the attraction. He wasn't looking for a wife, because she doubted he'd gotten over Nadine.

"Thank you." Bo whispered the words so softly that it took her a moment to figure out what he'd said. Before she could ask him what he was thanking her for, his phone rang again.

"It's O'Malley," he relayed to her. His phone was no longer on speaker, so Mattie couldn't hear what the sergeant was saying.

"How did that happen?" Bo asked, his voice rough and filled with the tone of the profanity he didn't use.

"No," Mattie mumbled. Please. She didn't want any more bad news.

She started to imagine the worst—that Arturo had learned the location of the safe house, and he was on the way there. She got to her feet in case they had to hurry out of there.

Bo stood, as well. "You're sure?" he asked O'Malley.

Bo obviously didn't like that response, either, because this time he spat out the profanity he'd held back earlier. "Bring him in. I want to talk to him."

That gave Mattie some hope. Had they actually caught Arturo? But those hopes were soon dashed.

"Arturo's dead," Bo let her know the moment he ended the call.

Part of her was relieved. The man wouldn't be coming to the safe house, and he couldn't make another attempt to kill her. "So we don't know who hired him?" she asked, already knowing the answer.

Bo shook his head. "He died on the scene without saying a word."

There was something he wasn't saying. "Died? How?"

"A shootout. Arturo was running a street over from where he attacked us, and when he was confronted, he tried to shoot his way out of it. Or so it seems."

"What do you mean? Did someone from SAPD shoot him?"

"No." And those jaw muscles stirred again. "Marshal Larry Tolivar killed Arturo."

"Tolivar? Why was he there?"

Bo shook his head. "I don't know, and it might take a while before we find out. Tolivar's not saying anything until his legal rep from the Justice Department shows up."

Chapter Thirteen

Bo practically rammed the keys into the ignition of the new unmarked car, the replacement vehicle for the one Arturo had shot to hell the day before. He was not in the right frame of mind to be questioning two suspects. One who was also a federal marshal and the other suspect, Kendall Collier, who might be behind all of this.

But he didn't have a choice.

While Bo would have preferred to stay at the safe house and have a long, relaxing breakfast with Mattie, Rosalie and the kids, this part of the investigation was too important for him to pawn it off on anyone else. Still, spending time with Mattie and the kids sounded like heaven.

And that troubled him a lot.

Lately, Mattie was part of every image that he had about his immediate future. She was there. Helping with the kids. Talking to him.

Adding something that hadn't been in his life for a long time. Yes, a big part of that *something* was sexual attraction, but he had the feeling that it could be a lot more than just that.

And that scared him.

Because to accept Mattie into his life meant he had to give up the old feelings he had for Nadine. Bo wasn't sure he was ready to do that.

"You okay?" Mattie asked, putting on her seat belt.

No. He wasn't. But Bo kept that to himself. Instead, he nodded, started the car and opened the garage door so he could back out.

"Your last chance," he mumbled. "You can stay here, and I can question Kendall and Tolivar on my own."

"I'm going," Mattie insisted. "I wouldn't have called Kendall and asked him to come to the station if I didn't plan to be there. He wants to talk to me, and I want to talk to him."

He checked her eyes to see if there was any doubt. There wasn't. But there was fatigue, and he was sure it was mirrored in his own eyes. It'd been a long night, and Mattie was likely still reeling from the shooting the day before—even though she managed to look amazing in the loaner purple dress that had been brought to the safe house for her. Thankfully, Bo kept several outfits in his office and had been able to use one of those, because he hadn't wanted to risk going back to his own house to get anything.

Because he thought they could both use it, he leaned over and put his mouth to hers. Bo had intended it to be something quick. Just a kiss of reassurance, but it was as effective as an hour of good foreplay. His body always seemed primed and ready when he was around Mattie.

"Do you think having sex would make us think better, as in clearing our heads?" The corner of Mattie's mouth lifted, and it made him wish she would smile more often. Of course, they didn't have a lot to smile about at the moment.

"Don't know about the thinking part," he drawled, kissing her again. "But it'd make us feel a hell of a lot better."

Since that wasn't a joke, Bo decided to end the torture and get to headquarters. Plus, it wasn't a good idea for them to be sitting in a garage kissing, especially when they had to discuss some things before they talked to their suspects.

"You shouldn't be in the room when I talk

with Tolivar," Bo said, and he continued even over her objection. "You can listen in and watch. You can even feed me questions if you think I'm missing something, but I have to do this interrogation by the book. We don't want his legal rep to step in and pull him away from our jurisdiction."

"They can do that?" she asked. No sign of that smile now. Reality was hitting her again.

"They can try." But Bo wanted to keep this within the SAPD so he could continue to have Mattie in his protective custody. If the feds took over the case, God knows what they would try to do in the name of protecting her.

"And now for Kendall," Bo said, moving on to their next problem. "I got a call about him this morning when you were in the shower. It's true. He really does have aplastic anemia. It's similar to leukemia, and he's stabilized with meds for now. But the only chance at a cure is a bone marrow donor."

"Holly," she mumbled.

"Holly," Bo confirmed. "Kendall could be so desperate to see if Holly's a match that he could be pretending to be a changed man." But Bo had to tell her the rest. "Or it could be for real. He did indeed sell his business, and he's had no recent association with anyone shady."

"That doesn't mean he's changed."

"No. But there's more. He's apparently working with the feds, the very people who arrested him for the illegal arms deal."

"He's what?"

Bo understood her shocked reaction because it was the same one he'd had when the captain told him the news. "The Justice Department won't give us details, only that Kendall is cooperating with them by giving them information about some of his former business associates. It's my guess that this deal will give him immunity, clear his name, and in turn the Justice Department will get to make some arrests."

She huffed. "And Kendall will go free."

Yes. And that could be a major problem, if Kendall was indeed the one who wanted Mattie dead. It might mean that Bo had to bargain with the devil, with Kendall, if there was any hope that Mattie would have a normal life. And her normalcy was necessary for Holly's.

Bo parked in the secure lot directly next to the headquarters building, and when they were done, he wouldn't use the same car to return to the safe house. He wanted to put as many layers of security as possible between this would-be killer and the children.

He led Mattie toward the interview room with the intention of starting with Tolivar, but he spotted Kendall in the hall outside his office. The man was alone, without his attorney or his fiancée. Kendall was leaning the back of his head against the wall, and he had his eyes closed. For just a brief second, Bo saw the man's fatigue, and Kendall no longer looked like the threat that he might possibly be.

That made him even more dangerous. He could be playing the part of a wolf in sheep's clothing.

"Kendall," Mattie said, practically snapping out his name.

Kendall's eyes flew open. He didn't offer them a smile or anything else friendly. "You wanted to see me."

Bo ushered them into his office so they'd have some privacy.

"I want to know the truth," Mattie said without even waiting until they were fully inside.

"The truth," Kendall repeated. "I wonder what that is myself."

Bo rolled his eyes. "Could we cut the existential BS and get to the facts? Mattie and

I want to know what you're really up to. And then you can tell us if you hired Arturo to try to kill her."

"I didn't hire him," Kendall said calmly. "But I can't rule out that someone did because they thought in some kind of warped way it would help me."

"Because if I'm dead, you'd be my daughter's next of kin," Mattie jumped in. "Well, I did an online will last night, and I've named Bo as her legal guardian. So, if I'm dead, you won't get your hands on her or her bone marrow."

Kendall nodded. "Good."

Surprised, Bo glanced at Mattie who obviously shared his reaction. "Good? Why?" she pressed.

"Because I don't want anyone with a reason to kill you. I know you don't believe that, but it's true."

"You're right," Mattie countered. "I don't believe that."

Bo wasn't sure he did, either, but it left him with a question. "Who would kill Mattie in order to help you?"

Kendall shrugged as if he might not answer, but he finally said, "Cicely. She wants me to live. That's why she insisted she get pregnant."

"You don't want the child?" Bo questioned.

Now, there was some emotion. Something flared through his eyes, but Kendall quickly concealed it. "I want the child," he insisted. "It's the mother I'm having second thoughts about."

So he didn't want to marry Cicely, but since she was carrying the baby that could ultimately save his life, Kendall was stuck with her. But Bo didn't feel sorry for the man. After all, Kendall could be the man who wanted Mattie dead.

"And then there's Ian," Kendall added after taking a deep breath. He looked Mattie straight in the eyes. "He could want to kill you for a different reason." He tipped his head to Bo. "And you're that reason."

Mattie made a sound of total disbelief. But Bo didn't. "Ian is jealous of me," Bo stated. "You think he's jealous enough to want me dead?"

"Maybe he wants both of you dead. Since he can't have Mattie, it's possible he might not want anyone to have her." Kendall paused. "I've been going over all of this for months. I didn't kill Mattie's fiancé, so that means someone else did."

Mattie folded her arms over her chest. "And

you think that someone is Ian?" She didn't wait for him to answer. "You're suggesting an old friend of yours could be guilty of some serious crimes, and you're apparently willing to do the same for your soon-to-be wife."

"If they're guilty, I want them to pay."

"Yeah," Bo grumbled. "And if they're arrested, then the guilt isn't on you."

"Believe what you will," Kendall said softly. He opened the door and started to leave.

But instead he practically ran into Cicely.

The woman looked as startled as Kendall did. But Bo saw something else in the depths of her eyes. She was angry. Had she heard Kendall's accusations?

"Why are you here?" Kendall asked Cicely.

"Because I love you. Because I was worried about you."

He didn't respond to that. He merely kissed her cheek. It was as chaste as the look he gave her. "I have an appointment. I'll see you at lunch." With that, he strolled away.

But Cicely didn't budge. "Did you agree to have your daughter tested for the bone marrow match?"

"No," Mattie answered.

"No?" It seemed as if all the breath left Cicely's body. "But why not? How could you have turned down Kendall at a time like this?"

"Kendall didn't ask," Bo informed her. And even if he had, the answer probably would have been no.

"He didn't?" Cicely was obviously dumbfounded. "He was supposed to ask." She shook her head. "But you'll agree to do it, right?"

"Bo and I will have to give that some thought," Mattie insisted.

"Thought? What's there to think about? You have a chance to save him, Mattie. You can't refuse. He's your own flesh and blood."

"He might have killed Brody," Mattie reminded her.

Cicely opened her mouth as if to vehemently deny that, but she closed it. She stood there for several long moments, apparently trying to figure out what argument she could give that would make Mattie change her mind.

"Don't you dare ruin my one chance at happiness," Cicely finally said, her voice clogged with emotion and with tears in her eyes.

Bo stepped closer, and he made sure the scowl on his face was a good one. "Is that a threat?"

Oh, Cicely clearly wanted to say that it was. But she was too smart for that. "No threat," she finally said.

Cicely reached into her purse and pulled out a business card, which she handed to Mattie. "Call me if you change your mind. Oh, and there's this…" She pulled out a small black jeweler's box that she gave Mattie, as well.

Mattie opened the box and Bo saw the diamond ring inside. Mattie shook her head. "What is this?"

"Ian found it in Brody's desk after he was killed. Apparently, Brody planned to give it to you."

"Oh." And that was all Mattie said.

Cicely shrugged. "I didn't think it was a good idea to give it to you, but Ian disagreed."

Mattie eased it into her pocket. "Thanks." And judging from her expression, she wasn't sure if it had been a good idea. It had definitely brought back some memories, and he could see the proof of that in her suddenly sad eyes.

"Think about having the test done," Cicely insisted. She walked away, hurrying in the direction where they'd last seen Kendall.

"Are you okay?" Bo asked Mattie.

She paused a moment. "I'm fine. The ring was just a surprise. When Brody proposed, he didn't have a ring yet. He said we would pick it out together, so I didn't know he'd even bought one." If she wanted to add anything to that, she dismissed it by clearing her throat and tipping her head to an exiting Cicely. "After conversations like the one we just had with her, I don't think we're any closer to the truth than we were when all of this started."

"Maybe." Bo waited for her to bring up the ring again. She didn't. So he decided to move on. "But we do have a lot of facts. Somewhere in all of that, there's the truth." But he was certainly beginning to suspect Cicely more and more. "Any reason Cicely would have been the one to have your fiancé killed?"

"Not directly." Now she paused. "But if she thought she was protecting Kendall…"

No need to finish that, because Bo was convinced that Cicely would do anything for Kendall. After all, she probably got pregnant to give him a possible bone marrow donor.

"I need to do the interview with Tolivar," he reminded her. "You can watch from the observation room and just text me if you have any questions."

They headed in that direction, but before they made it there, Bo saw his captain and Tolivar making their way up the hall toward him.

"There's been a change of plans," the

captain volunteered, and judging from his sour expression, this wasn't a good change for them.

Like his expression, Tolivar's stare was cold and hard. "My rep advised me to speak with my boss before I answer any of your questions."

Mattie huffed, and that was exactly how Bo felt. However, he didn't direct his comments to Tolivar but to his captain. "He shot and killed a man here in the city. It's our jurisdiction, and he should have to answer questions."

"Normally," the captain snarled.

"What the captain means is that Terrance Arturo was a suspect in a federal investigation. I was in pursuit of him when he took those shots at you. When he ran, I went after him. He turned, tried to kill me, so I took him out. Just as I'm trained to do."

"Yeah. But in doing so, you took out an assassin that someone had hired. By killing him you prevented us from learning the identity of his boss."

"I also saved him from coming after you again," Tolivar said directly to Mattie.

She nodded. "I'm grateful for that, but by killing Arturo the danger didn't end for me."

"No," Tolivar agreed. "And that's why I

wanted you back in my custody." His expression turned even harder. "But you've made your bed. Now you can sleep in it."

When the marshal started to walk away, Bo caught on to his arm. "What the hell does that mean?"

"It means I don't give a rat's you know what about Mattie, you or your situation. I was just trying to do my job, and look where the hell it got me." He threw off Bo's grip and walked away.

"What did he mean by that?" Mattie asked.

"Tolivar was suspended about a half hour ago," the captain explained.

"For shooting Arturo?" Bo wanted to know.

The captain shook his head. "We're not sure, and the Justice Department isn't talking. I'm thinking they want to pull him in because he botched this case."

Hell. Bo hoped that didn't mean some kind of cover-up. He wanted details about why Tolivar had been right there when Arturo launched that attack.

"Do we have any surveillance footage of the shootout between Arturo and the marshal?" Bo asked.

"We're working on it. If we get it and if

it shows Tolivar acted improperly when he killed Arturo, then somehow I'll haul his butt back in here."

Well, that was a start. "What do we do about Tolivar in the meantime?"

"Stay out of his path," the captain warned. "And watch your backs, because I wouldn't be surprised if Tolivar tried to get some revenge."

Chapter Fourteen

Mattie winced when the lightning shot through the sky. The storm had finally rolled in around midnight, and it wasn't showing any signs of letting up.

The thunder came, a low rumbling growl, and the rain pelted against the windowpanes. Thankfully, those were the only noises she heard. The safe house was quiet, and despite the storm, the children were sleeping. Rosalie had insisted on staying the night with them in the nursery, and even though Mattie had volunteered, as well, Bo had convinced her she should get some rest.

Right.

She was exhausted, and she'd managed to doze a little. Cat naps. If she could get her brain to settle down, she might get some honest-to-goodness sleep. But her thoughts kept going back to the danger. To the engagement ring she'd tucked into the dresser drawer. To the whole custody issue with Holly.

And to Bo.

Especially Bo.

There was another jolt of lightning, and Mattie resisted the urge to pull the covers over her head. That's what she would have done when she was a kid, but tonight she was already too warm, as if her skin were too tight. She recognized the feeling.

It was a pull, deep inside her. Probably some primitive response, she reasoned.

But the bottom line was she wanted Bo.

He was just next door, one room over, and she wanted to go to him. To climb into his bed with him. And do exactly what her body wanted her to do.

Mattie could only imagine what it would be like to be taken by a man like Bo. He always seemed right on the edge between danger and reason. Between being out of control and taking control.

What would it be like to have him inside her?

Moving, taking and not asking permission for whatever he chose to do to her?

Mattie could almost feel it, and it took the breath right out of her. She pressed her arms over her breasts, trying to stop the tingling that was making its way all over her body.

She saw movement through the open doorway of her room. Heard the footsteps. And then saw Bo. He was naked. Well, almost. He wore a pair of loose boxers that rode low on his hips. And he was aroused.

The boxers didn't hide that.

Was she just dreaming? Mattie was afraid so. She wanted to reach out and touch him, but he would no doubt disappear. So instead of trying to touch and losing the moment, she took her time, savoring the sight of him.

Outside the window another bolt of lightning slashed through the night and sent a spray of light over Bo's body. He was like something out of a fantasy.

All man and muscle.

His chest strong and welcoming. His face set in that expression she'd come to know so well. He looked ready to devour her.

Mattie smiled, still sleepy but now very alert. And very hot. "Are you here to devour me?" she asked, chuckling.

"If that's what you want," he drawled. He dropped his cell phone on the nightstand.

She froze. That didn't sound like a dream response. That sounded like the real thing.

Mercy.

If he was real, then no one deserved to look that good.

He stared at her, his eyes narrowing slightly. "I thought you'd be scared."

"I was." She swallowed hard. Not because she was afraid of the storm or what he might do next. Mattie was afraid he might go away.

But he didn't.

Bo reached down and jerked back the covers. She still had her hand on her breasts and probably looked like she was groping herself. However, she didn't have time to dwell on that. He moved forward, putting his knee on the bed. The mattress shifted with his weight, turning her toward him.

He leaned down, his mouth hovering over hers. His breath kissing her. He shoved aside her hand and put his own palm on her breast. "This is the only time I'll ask this—do you want me to leave?"

"No." She couldn't answer fast enough.

She reached for him, but Bo beat her to it.

His mouth came to hers, but not with the hard pressure she'd expected. No. He was almost gentle. Almost. His mouth barely touched, and it was the same with his tongue. But there was nothing gentle about his body.

His muscles were all corded as if he were fighting a fierce battle with himself.

With that same surprising gentleness, he moved the kisses to her cheek. To her neck. And then to her breasts, kissing her through the flimsy fabric of her cotton gown. Each touch of his mouth jabbed at the ache in the center of her body. Each time he ran his tongue over her nipples, the ache pierced through her until she arched her hips, looking for some kind of relief.

He cursed when she brushed against his erection.

Bo stared at her, his eyes hot and burning now. He grabbed her gown and pulled it over her head, sending it flying to the floor. He cursed again when he saw her panties and quickly rid her of those, too. He stripped them off her legs, but in the same motion he lowered his head and kissed her right in the center of all that heat.

Now Mattie cursed.

And when she arched her back, it wasn't to seek relief. This wasn't relief. His mouth was torture, and it nearly sent her straight to a climax.

She didn't want this to end so soon. She wanted it to last all night, but she would settle for at least a few more minutes. That wouldn't happen if he continued to kiss her there.

Mattie gripped his shoulders, pulling him up to her. More torture. Both of them were misted with sweat, and it created some sweet friction, with his firm male body sliding against hers.

"Could we do this now?" she asked, but it wasn't really a question. She fought to get his boxers off and then tried to position her body so that she could take him inside her.

But Bo had his own positioning ideas. He kissed her hard and rough this time. Just the way she wanted. The gentle foreplay had been nice, but she didn't want nice now. She wanted this hot alpha cop that she'd been lusting after for days.

Bo didn't disappoint. He latched on to her right leg, hooking it around his back. He did the same with her left one, and that put his hard sex right against hers.

Yes! Talk about living out a fantasy.

He kept kissing her, kept pressing his chest against her. And then he went inside her in one long stroke that filled her until she thought she might scream. She wasn't a screamer, but she might make an exception for this.

Her breath was gone, so she couldn't tell him how good it felt. She couldn't tell him that she was on fire. But Bo apparently knew that, because he moved in her, sliding against the right place to make that fire turn into an inferno.

Mattie fought to hang on, but the heat was too much. The need was too much.

And Bo knew exactly what he was doing.

He drove inside her, over and over again. So it didn't take much. A few of those strokes. Another kiss. And Mattie felt the gold light explode inside her head. Maybe it was the lightning. She doubted it, though. That gold light was from Bo. And she latched on to it. She latched on to him.

And she let herself shatter.

HELL.

That one word kept repeating through Bo's mind. He was in trouble.

Being with Mattie had been far better than his expectations, and he'd expected something pretty damn amazing.

Because his body wasn't on fire right now and had just been sated, he wanted to dismiss this visit to her bed as bad judgment. He could have even lumped it together as a reaction to all the stress they'd been under.

Yeah. "Stress sex." Good name for it.

Hell.

He wasn't even sure it'd been just sex. It felt a lot more like making love, and that caused him to mentally curse again. He knew better than to get involved with Mattie. She already had too much to deal with, and now he'd added himself to the things she had to work out. Because she was no doubt trying to put this in its proper place just as he was doing.

He braced himself for the talk. The one where she would make him feel like dirt for adding this wrinkle to her life.

But she didn't say a word.

Mattie made a sound of sleepy pleasure, a sort of low feminine moan, and her eyes drifted closed.

She fell asleep.

Bo stared at her, watching her face, waiting. But after a few minutes, it was clear she wasn't in the mood for talking.

Relieved, and a little confused, he rolled off her so his weight wouldn't crush her. Without opening her eyes, she adjusted, wiggling her body against him until she was on her side facing him, her breasts squished against his chest.

She made another of those sounds of sleepy pleasure.

Maybe because she was thinking about her late fiancé?

That put a scowl on his face. Because he sure hadn't been thinking about Nadine when he'd been inside Mattie.

He was right back to mumbling *hell* again.

Bo pushed her hair from her face and brushed a good-night kiss off her forehead.

"Bo," she mumbled, using the same tone as her sleepy pleasure sounds.

The way she said his name, it went through him like a shot of expensive whiskey. Smooth and warm. It made him want to take her all over again. And he might have done just that.

If his phone hadn't beeped.

He had changed the ring tone so it wouldn't wake everyone if he got a midnight call. And that's apparently what he'd gotten.

Bo reached over, retrieved his phone and checked the caller ID screen. It was Sergeant O'Malley and therefore a call he had to take.

He got out of the bed, moving away from Mattie's warm body. His own body protested the loss right away, and he promised himself he would go back to her when he finished.

"Don't give me bad news," Bo whispered to the sergeant. He went into the adjoining bathroom so he could talk.

"Not this time. We just got a call from a tech over in the Justice Department. Because of the nonstop attempts to kill Mattie, they've been working night and day to see if they can figure out who hacked into the Witness Protection database."

"And?" Bo asked.

"And we have a winner. It's Terrance Arturo."

Arturo. A dead guy who used to work for Kaplan and Collier. "Is there proof?"

"Just some notes found in Arturo's apartment. Don't worry. We'll keep digging. The captain's here, and he just brought in Collier, Cicely Carr and Kaplan for questioning. Tolivar's boss has agreed to bring him, as well."

Since it was midnight, he was betting all of them were especially riled with the timing and the subject of this interrogation. "I'll get dressed and get down there."

"No. The captain says for you to stay put. But he thinks by morning, he'll know who was behind the attempts to kill Mattie and you."

Chapter Fifteen

The voices and sounds woke her.

Mattie's eyes flew open, and she was stunned to see that it was daylight. The rain was still spattering against the windows, but there was no hint of lightning or thunder. The worst of the storm had passed.

She glanced at the clock and couldn't believe the time. It was 8:00 a.m., and even though that was still early to a lot of people, it obviously wasn't for Jacob and Holly, because it was their voices she was hearing.

Mercy, she hadn't expected to sleep at all, much less for eight straight hours.

She threw back the cover and caught Bo's scent still on the sheets. On her, too. It made her feel all warm and golden again. But then she sighed. Yes, it was great sex, but Bo was probably having trouble coming to terms with it. Mattie was surprised to realize that she wasn't having doubts or issues. It was crystal clear to her.

She cared deeply for Bo and wanted him in her life.

However, working that out was an entirely different matter. Bo might not be ready for an emotional entanglement, especially since he already had enough entanglements in his life.

She took a quick shower and dressed in another of the loaner outfits that she grabbed from the closet—a dark red cotton dress and a pair of black flats. Mattie slapped on some makeup and tried not to think about how awkward it would be to face Bo. She only thought about facing Jacob and Holly and hoped she wasn't too late to share breakfast with them.

Mattie hurried into the kitchen and came to a stop. Bo was at the stove cooking, his back to her, and he had his phone anchored between his ear and shoulder. Rosalie was wrestling with Jacob, trying to get him strapped into the high chair. Holly was already in her chair, and the little girl gave Mattie a bright smile.

These were the things she'd dreamed of seeing for the past thirteen months, and here was her baby, right in front of her.

Jacob smiled, too, when he saw her and quit

struggling with Rosalie, who quickly put him in the chair.

"Sorry about all the noise," Rosalie said, "I was trying to keep them quiet."

"I'm glad they woke me." Mattie wouldn't have wanted to miss this for the world. She went closer and helped Rosalie put some dry cereal bits on the trays. Mattie knew this part of the routine. The kids would eat the cereal while Bo prepared a hot breakfast. This morning, it was oatmeal. Bo was stirring a pot of it on the stove as he added some brown sugar.

"He's been on that phone since the kids got up," Rosalie remarked, dishing up some of the oatmeal into two different bowls.

The nanny handed Mattie one of them after adding some milk to cool it down. Apparently, she was going to get to feed her daughter this morning.

But Mattie gave some of her attention to Bo. She couldn't tell who he was talking to, but judging from his stiff body language, it was about the investigation.

Mattie pulled up a chair and gave Holly the first spoonful of oatmeal. Most of it made it into her mouth. However, Holly took part of that bite into her hand and squished it around her fingers.

All right. So breakfast would be messy.

But fun. Holly babbled with each bite and even offered Mattie some from her fingers. Mattie gladly sampled it and then did the same for Jacob, who obviously wanted to be included.

She loved them both so much and wondered just how much it would break her heart if she couldn't have all of them—Bo, Holly, Jacob and even Rosalie—in her life.

Bo ended the call, closing the phone and shoving it into his pocket. He looked ready for work in his black pants and white dress shirt. He'd even shaved, making her wonder if he'd gotten any sleep whatsoever.

"Sorry I didn't get up sooner," she said to him. She'd been right about the awkward part. "I slept like a rock."

He smiled a little, just enough to ease some of her anxiety and to renew the heat that always flared whenever she was around him.

"That was my captain on the phone," he explained, the smile fading. "When they searched Arturo's apartment, they found notes that indicate he's the one who hacked into the database of the Witness Protection Program."

She tried not to react, because Holly was only inches away, but it was impossible to keep her emotions totally in check. Arturo. He had been the one who had started the spiral of danger that had ultimately caused her to leave Holly in the hospital with Nadine.

"Any idea why he outed my location and identity?" Mattie asked.

Obviously sensing the seriousness of the conversation, Rosalie took over feeding duties, and Mattie stood so she could face Bo.

"Arturo probably did it for money. There's about twenty thousand dollars of unaccounted funds in his bank account."

So, for twenty grand he had compromised the lives of her and Holly. If he weren't already dead, Mattie would have gone after him for that. Of course, that left her with the big question. "Who paid him?"

Bo shook his head. "Still trying to figure that out. Detectives have been going through his apartment all night, and they found a key that appears to be to a safety deposit box. They're trying to figure out now where the box is located so they can get into it."

Good. Because maybe there was proof of his boss's identity, and that meant Bo could soon make an arrest.

"The captain had Kendall, Cicely and Ian all in for questioning," Bo added.

"During the night?"

"Most of the night," he clarified. "He just released them about a half hour ago."

Well, Mattie would hear about it, that was for certain. They were all probably fuming, especially since none of them thought the police had a right to consider them suspects. "What about Marshal Tolivar? Did the captain manage to question him, too?"

"Not yet. But he's having a meeting first thing this morning with Tolivar's boss."

More good news, because maybe they would finally get the truth about the marshal. "So we have to go back to headquarters?" Mattie asked.

"Not just yet. I thought you deserved a quiet morning."

Holly chose that moment to let out a squeal when she couldn't get a glob of oatmeal out of her hair.

"Time for baths," Rosalie announced. She put the oatmeal bowls aside, and Bo helped her get the children out of the high chairs.

"Need help?" Mattie asked the nanny.

"No thanks. Bo and you probably have some things to discuss anyway." Rosalie smiled in such a way that Mattie wondered if the woman knew what had happened between them last night.

Rosalie carried the babies out, one snuggled

in each arm, and just like that, the kitchen went from being very noisy to totally silent. Since Mattie wasn't sure what to say, she settled for pouring herself a glass of orange juice and sitting on one of the bar stools at the counter. Bo poured himself some coffee.

And the silence continued.

"Sorry I fell asleep on you last night," she mumbled.

More silence. And then he walked toward her and dropped a kiss on her lips. "Actually, I was the one on you." He smiled, and that made everything instantly better.

"I was worried about you," she admitted. "I wasn't sure how you'd handle the after part."

"I wasn't sure, either," Bo admitted. "But I decided—"

His phone rang, and both of them cursed under their breath. He glanced at the caller ID screen before he answered. "O'Malley," he greeted.

Mattie figured this call was important, but she hated that the sergeant hadn't waited several more seconds so she could have heard what Bo was about to say.

"He did what?" Bo asked, his voice suddenly as intense as his expression. "Why?"

Mattie couldn't hear a word of what the

sergeant was saying, but she wasn't getting a good feeling about this. Mercy. What was going on now?

"Does the search warrant cover that?" Bo asked, and a moment later he huffed. "All right." He paused. "I'd rather not do it that way, though."

Bo met Mattie's gaze, and she could tell he was trying to reassure her, but it wasn't working.

"Let's go with Plan B," Bo continued, still talking to O'Malley. "Yeah, that with heavy security. Oh, and you said she'll need a photo ID that the bank officials will verify with their security service. No fakes. This needs to be a real ID in case it has to stand up in court. No repeats of what happened with the federal investigation into Collier's case. Someone needs to print her another copy of her driver's license."

It was impossible to tell exactly what was going on from just hearing Bo's side of the conversation. Were they talking about her?

"Okay. That sounds good," Bo finally said to O'Malley. "We'll leave just as soon as an officer arrives to stay here with the kids."

She set her juice aside. "What's wrong?" Mattie asked when he ended the call.

Bo scrubbed his hand over his face. "The

key they found in Arturo's apartment was indeed for a safety deposit box at a bank downtown."

"And the search warrant doesn't allow you to search that deposit box?" She'd been able to gather that much from what she'd heard.

"No. It's a foreign bank, and they're insisting the search warrant isn't valid because there are two names on the account. Arturo's and yours."

Mattie was so glad she wasn't holding the juice glass, or she would have dropped it. "Mine? Why would Arturo put my name on his deposit box?"

Bo shook his head. "We might not know that until we get a look at what's in that box. This bank's going to stonewall a search warrant for hours, but you should be able to get into the box right away."

She was already getting to her feet, but she was also trying to figure out why this had happened. "How soon will the officer be here?"

"He's already out front. We had a car patrolling all night, so he was just up the block." Bo walked around the counter. "I'll tell Rosalie what's going on."

Mattie followed him so she could say goodbye to the children. Hopefully, this wouldn't be a long trip, and maybe, just maybe, there was something in that safety deposit box to tell them who was trying to kill them.

Of course, they could get more than that. Mattie remembered what had happened the last time they were downtown.

Arturo had tried to kill them.

She and Bo kissed the children and headed out to the garage once Bo let the other officer inside. Mattie didn't voice her concern until they were in the car.

"What if this is a trap?" she asked. "What if Arturo set it up so that if he were killed, then this would draw me out in the open?"

"I thought of that. That's why we're going with Plan B. We'll send in a female detective wearing a hat and dark glasses. I'll be with her. The idea is if anyone is watching, they'll think it's you."

"And where will I be?"

"Safe with two detectives in the building next door to the bank. If all goes well, then we'll take you into the bank so you can get into that box."

"With my newly printed driver's license?" she questioned.

"Yeah. No repeats of what happened with Kendall. Evidence that would have convicted him was thrown out because the FBI didn't execute a proper search of his office and files. I want to be able to use anything incriminating in that box to make an arrest and to prosecute this SOB."

Mattie couldn't agree more. She nodded. "Let's do this."

Bo nodded, too, but he didn't move. He sat there, looking at her. And then he leaned over and kissed her. It was smooth and gentle. Probably for reassurance. But Bo's kisses only reassured her that she wanted him. They did the opposite of calming her down.

"Hold that thought," he mumbled against her lips. "And tonight, I want you to come to my bed."

Like the kiss, that invitation warmed her to the bone. So, it wouldn't be just a one-night stand between them, but Mattie didn't want to think beyond that. One step at a time.

Without taking his eyes off her, Bo started the engine, and he pressed the remote control on the visor to open the garage door. Mattie braced herself for another kiss, another assault on her senses. She wasn't, however, prepared for her door to fly open.

It happened so fast, she didn't have time to think or react.

Something came flying at her. A canister of some kind.

And it exploded.

Chapter Sixteen

Bo caught just a glimpse of the person dressed all in black, and in that glimpse he saw the silver canister that the guy hurled into the car.

That glimpse was all Bo got.

Something began to spew from the can, and it created an instant fog. Bo's eyes watered to the point that he couldn't see, and he began to cough uncontrollably. Tear gas.

Beside him, he heard Mattie coughing, as well. And struggling. She seemed to be fighting something, though Bo couldn't tell what. He drew his gun and reached for her, trying to pull her closer so he could try to protect her. What he couldn't do was shoot, because he had no idea where to aim. For all practical purposes, he was blind.

Bo blinked hard, trying to focus, and he used his left hand to open his door. The garage door was already open, and he was hoping the ventilation and the falling rain would clear out the tear gas. But it wouldn't happen immediately. And that meant he somehow had to get Mattie out of there.

Still coughing and unable to catch his breath, Bo latched on to Mattie's arm and pulled hard, trying to yank her out on his side of the car. It didn't work, and Bo knew why.

Someone was trying to pull her out the other side.

Bo hadn't seen the person, probably because the guy had stayed low and slipped in the moment Bo opened the garage door. Of course, it hadn't helped that Bo had also been kissing Mattie, and that had given this SOB the time to launch an attack.

Later, Bo would curse himself for the lapse in judgment. But for now, he had to save Mattie. He also had to pray there was just one attacker. Because if there were others, he might not be able to stop this.

Whatever *this* was.

If it were an assassination attempt, then why hadn't the guy just shot them when he had the chance? Why not just shoot now? That was yet something else he'd have to figure out later.

Bo pulled harder, trying to drag Mattie toward him. She still didn't budge, but he heard her gasping for air and struggling. She was fighting the guy, but like Bo, she probably couldn't see a thing, and without air in her lungs, her fight would be weak at best.

Bo considered yelling out to the officer inside, but that was too big a risk to take. This could all be a ruse to get inside the safe house so that someone could kidnap Holly. Bo couldn't take that risk, and he knew without a doubt that Mattie wouldn't want him to take it, either.

Since this tug-of-war wasn't working, Bo stumbled from the car and tried to pull in as much fresh air as he could. The tear gas had created a thick, misty fog in the car itself, but it wasn't confined just to the car. It was all around, making him wonder if their attacker had opened another canister on the garage floor. If so, this had been a well-planned attack. But it left him with one nasty question.

How had this person found the location of the safe house?

Bo had locked the door that led from the garage into the house. He was sure of that. He was also sure that the officer would have reset the security alarm. But alarms weren't going to help them if this guy decided to get inside the house.

Bo somehow managed to stay on his feet, though each breath and each step were a struggle. Still, he didn't give up. He had to get to the other side of the car so he could help Mattie.

He made it to the back of the car, using the vehicle itself to help support his weight. Without it, he would have dropped to his knees and given in to the coughing fit.

Bo tried to shout out a warning, but that failed, too, so he lifted his gun and took aim at the dark figure that was trying to drag Mattie out of the car. When there was a break in the mist, Bo saw something else.

The guy was wearing a military-style gas mask.

"Stop!" Bo finally managed to say.

But the person didn't. Their attacker grabbed Mattie's hair and pulled her partially out. In the same motion, he put a gun to her head.

Mattie was still struggling, still trying to say something, and pulling back. She was trying to get away from the person with the gun. But Bo only concentrated on the guy wearing the gas mask. It could be Tolivar, Ian or Kendall. Hell, it could even be Cicely.

Or a hired gun.

Whatever the case, this situation was as

dangerous as it got, because the person was using Mattie as a human shield.

"Let her go," Bo tried to say.

The guy clearly had no intention of doing that. Bo expected him to try to run.

He didn't.

With the gun still pressed to Mattie's head, the guy said something to her. Something that Bo couldn't hear, but whatever it was, just like that, she stopped struggling.

Hell. What was going on?

That question didn't stay unanswered for long. Because the guy crawled over Mattie.

"Stop!" Bo yelled again.

But it didn't do any good. The guy got behind the wheel and threw the car into Reverse.

He came right at Bo.

Bo had to dive, fast, out of the way, so he wouldn't be run over. He hit the concrete floor hard, landing on his shoulder. The pain shot through him, but he somehow managed to hang on to his gun.

For all the good it would do.

He still didn't have a clean shot.

With the tires squealing and kicking up smoke, the gunman peeled out of the garage and driveway. He was getting away.

With Mattie.

Bo's eyes were still watering, so he couldn't see clearly, but he took aim at the rear tire. The blast would no doubt alert everyone inside, and he prayed the officer would keep everything locked up and secure.

Bo fired, and the bullet ripped through the tire. But it was too little, too late.

Because the driver gunned the engine and sped away despite the flat tire.

He tried to blink away the rain and the remnants of the tear gas, and he started running. Somehow he had to get Mattie out of that vehicle. God knows what this man was planning to do to her.

Bo fired another shot at the other rear tire. This time, the bullet hit the rim. He saw the spark of metal against metal, and Bo's heart went to his knees.

The gunman just kept on going, quickly eating up the distance between Mattie and him. Bo saw her terrified expression before the car disappeared around the corner.

MATTIE COULDN'T CATCH her breath, and she felt on the verge of a panic attack. The tear gas or whatever had been in that canister was responsible, but she knew she had to fight off the effects or she was going to die.

She caught a glimpse of Bo in the mirror

and watched as he fired another shot. He was aiming for the car's tires, she was sure of that. But even though at least one tire seemed to be damaged, the driver wasn't stopping.

Mattie reached for the door handle. Her captor was driving fast, and the car was shaking from the now-flat tire, but she couldn't wait and hope that he would slow down. She had to get out of there now before he managed to get her away from Bo and the safe house.

"Move and I'll shoot," the man growled. She heard him but didn't recognize his voice. Of course, he could be disguising it. "If I have to kill you, I'll go back for your kid."

Mattie froze. She couldn't stop herself from reacting to that threat. Maybe because her adrenaline and anxiety levels were through the roof. Logically, she knew that Bo would do whatever it took to keep this goon from getting anywhere near Holly.

But Bo could die trying to protect her daughter.

She'd caught a final glimpse of Bo before the gunman sped away. He looked enraged. Mattie was furious, too. How had this man gotten close enough to kidnap her in broad daylight?

Her head was pounding now, and the sound of the tire slapping against the asphalt didn't help. She needed to think clearly, but instead she was a mess. Her eyes and throat were on fire, and she couldn't pull in a decent breath.

"Who are you?" she asked, but even saying just those few words caused her to cough almost uncontrollably.

"That's not your concern. Right now, the only thing you have to do is sit there and shut up."

No. She needed to do a lot more than that. Bo would try to come for her, Mattie was certain of that, but she couldn't count on him or anyone else reaching her in time. She had to save herself.

"Where are you taking me?" she demanded. Mattie looked all around her to see if there was anything inside the vehicle that she could grab and use as a weapon. Her purse was on the floor. She might be able to hit him with it.

"I said shut up," he snarled.

He ripped off his gas mask and tossed it onto the back seat. Mattie got a good look at him then. He had dark brown hair and eyes.

And he was a stranger.

He'd been hired to kidnap her. Maybe even to kill her.

Mattie's heart sank. If this had been Kendall,

Ian or Cicely, she could perhaps reason with them. Perhaps even with Tolivar. But how did you reason with a man who was likely doing this for money?

"Whatever you're being paid, I can pay you more," she tried.

The man jammed the gun against her head. "I said shut up."

So much for her attempt to bribe him. Mattie cleared her throat after another round of coughing and kept watch, waiting for a chance to escape.

He drove out of the subdivision and took a right on the main highway. She knew it would eventually lead them to the interstate, where there'd be lots of traffic. Certainly someone would see the gun pointed at her head or the flat tire and report it to the cops. There was also the fact that they were in an unmarked police car.

It probably had GPS tracking.

The relief flooded through her. Bo would be able to find her. But she still wasn't giving up on her own attempts to escape. She would just need to wait until the driver was distracted. A few seconds was all she needed. And she could open the door and jump out. He would fire at her, of course, so that meant she had to pray that she wasn't injured in the fall. She would need to be able to run.

Each second that he drove clicked off in her head, and she finally saw the sign for the interstate.

But he didn't take it.

The gunman drove right past it and took a right turn. He drove about a mile before he came to a stop behind a dark blue truck. This wasn't a residential area but rather a street lined with warehouses that were spaced far apart. There wasn't another person in sight.

He turned to her and jammed the gun even harder against her head. "I'm only going to say this one time. Cooperate or you die. I get paid whether I deliver you dead or alive."

Mattie had no idea if that were true, but if his boss didn't mind her dead, then why hadn't he just killed her in the garage? He certainly had had the element of surprise and could have fired a couple of shots before she even knew what hit her.

So, who wanted to keep her alive?

And why?

"Come on," the gunman insisted. "We're getting in that truck."

Oh, God. If he managed to get her in that vehicle, then there might not be any way for Bo and the cops to track where he was taking her.

"I said come on," he growled.

He latched on to her hair again and dragged her across the seat toward him. The pain shot through her. So did the fear. He was a lot bigger than she was. Stronger, too. Plus, he had a gun, and she didn't. But Mattie knew she couldn't give in to that fear.

She had to do something now.

She'd had some martial arts training when she became a P.I., and she would rely on that. She prayed it would be enough. If she could just get away and run back to the main highway, someone would be able to help her.

With the gunman still pulling at her, Mattie went limp.

Because he had hold of her and because he was so strong, she went flying at him. Mattie lowered her head and aimed for his chest. She rammed into him, sending them both crashing to the rain-slick pavement.

She tried to get up, but he used his strength to keep her pinned to the ground.

"Stop it," he growled right against her ear. "Or I make one phone call. Just one. And a sniper will start shooting in the safe house. He won't stop until he's killed everyone inside. Got that?"

Mattie stopped struggling. Yes, she wanted

to live. She wanted to raise her daughter, but she couldn't risk Holly, Jacob and Rosalie's safety so that she could live. That's the reason she had walked away from the hospital thirteen months ago. She hadn't waited this long only to put her baby right back in danger.

"That's more like it." He got up and jerked her to her feet.

The rain whipped at them. It was coming down harder now, and she hoped that would slow him down a little.

It didn't.

He didn't waste any time. With a firm grip on her, he hurried to the truck. It was unlocked, so he opened the door and crammed her inside. The moment he was in, he pressed the button to engage the locks. That's when Mattie noticed she didn't even have a lock on her side of the truck. The lock button and the door handle itself had been ripped off.

She was trapped.

The gunman started the engine and jammed his foot on the accelerator. The truck bolted forward, the tires digging into the mud on the soft shoulder. But that barely slowed him down. He raced down the side street and past the warehouses.

Mattie watched the side mirror as they sped

away. When the unmarked car was no longer in sight, she knew her chances for rescue had just gone from slim to none.

Chapter Seventeen

The wipers slashed across the windshield, clearing the rain that was coming down hard now, but it wasn't clearing it fast enough for Bo. He needed to hurry, and the rain and slick roads were slowing him down.

So was the GPS tracker.

He was getting the tracking feed from a computer at headquarters, and it was being transmitted to his phone. But it seemed to be moving at a snail's pace. The red blip on the screen was cruising along, only to disappear for a few seconds. When it popped back up, it was blocks ahead of where he'd been on the previous image. If the transmission had a delay at the wrong time, he might miss a turn and have to double back.

His heart was pounding hard enough to hurt his ribs. The tear gas was still giving his eyes and throat some problems. But those were all minor annoyances. The only thing that mattered now was getting to Mattie in time.

From the moment he'd seen the gas-masked goon driving off with her, Bo had had a split-second debate with himself. Part of him wanted to rush after Mattie, but he also knew he had to keep the children safe. He couldn't be sure this wasn't a trick to draw him away from the house. That's why he'd taken the time to call for other officers, not for his own backup, but he wanted a team of detectives guarding the house. When he was certain they were on their way and only minutes out, he'd jumped into the officer's unmarked patrol car and sped after the gunman and Mattie.

He had to get to her in time.

God knows what this kidnapper had in mind, but Bo didn't think the outcome would be good for Mattie.

Was Kendall or Ian behind this? Or Cicely? Maybe they planned to hold Mattie captive so that she would agree to have Holly tested as a bone marrow donor. That seemed extreme, but these were people who had dealt in extremes before.

Bo cursed when the blip disappeared again. His chest was pumping now, and every nerve inside him was primed and ready for a fight. What he needed was his opponent, and for that to happen he had to see where the gunman was taking Mattie.

The red blip jumped back onto the screen, and Bo saw the getaway car's turn. Hell. He had to slam on his brakes and then hope like the devil that he didn't go into a skid. He'd be of no help to Mattie if he crashed. He took the turn on what had to be two wheels, and fought with the steering wheel to regain control.

Then his phone rang.

That cut the tracking feed images.

He saw the captain's number appear on the screen, but Bo only wanted it to go away so he could get back to finding the car.

"I need you off the line," Bo said, answering the call.

"I know. Because you're getting the GPS coordinates. But I can give them to you while I see if I can talk you into waiting for backup."

"Not a chance. I'm finding Mattie."

"That's what I figured you'd say, but I had to try. Keep going straight. The car's just ahead." The captain paused. "It's not moving, Bo."

That nearly knocked the breath right out of him. If the car wasn't moving, that meant God knows what could be happening to Mattie.

The gunman could be trying to kill her.

Bo slammed his foot on the accelerator and

spotted the car on the side of the road. He tried to see what was going on inside, but the rain made that impossible. He pulled up behind the car, slamming on his brakes, and he jumped out before his vehicle even stopped moving.

He drew his gun, took aim and approached the car.

His heart dropped.

Because the car was empty.

Empty!

He hurried back to grab his cell phone. "She's not here. No one is." Bo glanced around at all the warehouses. There were dozens of them, and the gunman could have taken her in any one of them.

Except why would he park back here, a good twenty yards from the nearest one? Why not just park closer?

"I have officers on the way there to look for her," the captain told Bo.

Bo heard him but didn't respond. That's because something caught his attention. Something off on the shoulder of the road, dug into the mud.

Tire tracks.

And they were very recent, because the rain hadn't washed them away yet.

The gunman had ditched the unmarked car

and moved her to another vehicle. Bo cursed. There was no way to follow her now.

Or was there?

The road was just two lanes and fairly narrow, so he hurried to the other side. No tracks there, which meant the gunman hadn't made a U-turn and gone back out to the highway. He'd driven straight ahead.

"Get the officers out to Industrial Road," Bo told the captain. He raced back to his car, got inside and gunned the engine. "And see if you can get any kind of surveillance feed from one of these warehouses. Based on those tire tracks, I think we're looking for a heavy vehicle, probably an SUV or truck."

"We're on the way," the captain assured him. "But we'll do a silent approach. All unmarked cars. We don't want this guy panicking."

Neither did Bo. Because that was the fastest way to get Mattie killed.

"Where does this road lead?" Bo asked.

"Nowhere. It's a dead end. But there are two smaller roads that feed off it. One is about a half mile up on your right. The other, about a mile to your left. The one on the right just leads to more warehouses, but the one on the left will take you back to the highway."

And the gunman could be on either.

If Mattie's attacker planned to kill her

right away or hand her over to someone else, that could happen in one of the more remote warehouses. However, if he wanted to get her out of the area, then he would head back to the highway because that in turn would take him to the interstate. If the gunman made it that far, it would be next to impossible to find Mattie.

Bo shoved his phone in his pocket so he could concentrate on the drive and so he could keep his gun ready. He flew past the warehouses, taking notice of each of the parking lots. There were some semis, but he was pretty sure he wasn't looking for that type of vehicle.

He slowed down when he approached the turn on the right. The turn that would lead to more warehouses and a dead end. It wasn't the turn he thought the gunman would take.

But Bo saw the dark blue truck.

It was the right size to have made those tire tracks in the mud, and it was parked at an odd angle in the side parking lot of one of the warehouses. Next to it was a black car.

His gut told him Mattie was in one of those vehicles.

Bo didn't slam on his brakes because it would make too much noise and possibly alert her kidnapper. Instead, he came to a stop and backed up so he could turn into the road. He didn't speed, though it was next to impossible to keep himself from doing just that. Bo wanted to make it look as if he were headed there on business. Maybe as a worker at one of the warehouses. He wanted the element of surprise on his side.

As Bo approached the truck, he kept his focus straight ahead, but he studied the truck from the corner of his eye.

Mattie.

He was both relieved and terrified to see her in the cab of the truck. She was alive, but the guy had a gun jammed against her head.

It took everything inside Bo to keep driving. If he stopped now, the gunman would likely just shoot her point-blank. Bo had to figure out a way to stop that from happening.

He turned into the parking lot of the next warehouse. He couldn't see the truck from that angle, which was good, because it meant the gunman couldn't see him. Bo jumped out of his car and started running toward the back of the warehouse. His best bet was to try to sneak up on them.

The rain beat at him, and he had to wipe the drops from his face just to see. Still, he didn't slow down because his gut was telling him something else—he didn't have much time.

It seemed to take forever, but he finally reached the far corner of the warehouse. He stopped and peered around the corner.

Hell.

He was right about not having much time. The gunman had Mattie out of the truck, and he was dragging her toward the parked black car. Someone was already inside that vehicle, but Bo couldn't see the person's face.

He could certainly see Mattie's and the gunman's faces, though. Mattie was frightened, but she was also fighting to stop herself from being taken to that black car. But the gunman was fighting, too. He kept his weapon pointed at her head while he muscled her toward the other vehicle.

The trunk of the black car popped open. Someone inside had obviously used an interior button to do that. And the trunk was where the gunman was trying to force her to go.

"Stop fighting me!" the man yelled. He slammed his gun against the side of Mattie's head. He was a stranger. And about to be a dead one.

The rage roared through Bo, and even though he knew the person in the car could take a shot at him, he couldn't just stand there and let Mattie be beaten by this thug.

Bo came out of cover and took aim so he could fire a warning shot over the gunman's head. He wanted nothing more than to put a bullet in this guy, but Bo couldn't risk that with Mattie in the man's grip.

He fired the shot, and just as Bo had hoped, her attacker pivoted in Bo's direction. What the man didn't do was let go of Mattie. He slung her in front of him.

"Drop you gun and let her go," Bo ordered.

For a split second, Mattie's eyes met Bo's. The rain was sheeting down her face, and she was pale, but he saw something he hadn't seen earlier when she was in the other vehicle.

Determination.

She wasn't going to just stand there and let this kidnapper kill her.

Mattie threw her weight to the right, landing with a thud against the black car. And even though her attacker didn't let go of her, there was just enough space for Bo to get off a clean shot.

He took it.

The gunman aimed his weapon at Bo. He wasn't nearly fast enough. Bo double tapped the trigger, sending two bullets right into the man.

Her attacker dropped to the ground, his weapon skittering across the wet concrete.

He watched the guy on the ground to make sure he wasn't faking his death. Bo didn't want this SOB going for the gun. But he also had another matter: the black car.

"Move away from the car," Bo told Mattie.

But it was already too late.

The car door flew open, and someone inside grabbed Mattie and dragged her into the car.

Chapter Eighteen

It took a moment for Mattie to register that someone had hold of her and had pulled her onto the driver's seat. She was literally sitting on someone's lap. Her attention had been on the gunman. The man who'd kidnapped her and threatened her life.

He was now dead on the ground.

Bo had shot him. Bo had saved her.

She hadn't had time to feel the relief or run to Bo. Because someone had her again.

Mattie fought to break free of the grip, but then her new attacker pressed something over her face. A cloth. And because Mattie was already breathing hard, she drew in the sick-sweet smell.

Chloroform.

She recognized the scent from a case she'd worked on early in her career. Someone was trying to knock her out.

Mattie rammed her elbow against that

someone and made contact. The person gasped and loosened the grip just a little on the cloth. Even though Mattie was already feeling the effects of the drug, she elbowed the person again and again.

Until her attacker dropped the cloth.

However, she didn't have time to get out of the car because an arm curved around her neck, and someone jammed a gun against her head. Again.

"Mattie?" Bo called out.

He was moving closer to the car, and he had his gun aimed. Mattie could see that much, though her vision was blurry. Everything was swimming in and out of focus. Including her ability to concentrate. She cursed the chloroform and her attacker. She needed a clear head if both she and Bo were going to get out of this alive.

"Move and I'll kill him," her attacker growled against her ear.

It was a man, and even though her head was too fuzzy to recognize the hoarse whisper, she understood what he was threatening. He would kill Bo.

Mattie stopped struggling. She stopped fighting. She just sat there and drew in some deep breaths, hoping it would help her think better.

What could she do to stop this?

Bo walked closer, and he didn't take his attention off her and her attacker. He stepped to the side of the car, by the open door, and his eyes widened when he looked inside.

"Let her go," Bo warned.

Was he talking to another hired gun, or was that recognition she saw on Bo's face?

"Step out of the car and put down your gun. You're not going to get away with this," Bo tried again.

"I already have," the man fired back.

She lost what little breath she'd managed to regain. That's because Mattie recognized the voice. This wasn't a hired gun or a stranger.

It was Ian.

Ian was the one holding the gun to her head. And he was no doubt the one who'd hired the dead man to kidnap her from the safe house.

"How did you find me?" she asked.

"The ring."

She was surprised that he gave an answer, any answer. But she shook her head. "What ring?"

"The one I had Cicely give you. Your old engagement ring. Well, a fake one, anyway. Brody didn't leave that in his desk. I bought it and put a tiny tracking device in the bottom of the box. It worked. It led me right to you."

Ian moved his mouth closer to her ear. "I would have had my man there sooner, but I got held up at police headquarters and couldn't call him. I was there most of the night. If not, this would all be over by now."

Over. Oh, God. "What do you want?" Mattie asked.

Ian brushed a kiss on her cheek. "I want you, of course."

His words and the touch of his mouth on her skin turned her stomach. Was he insane, or was this some kind of sick attempt to help Kendall?

Mattie looked at Bo to see what she could read from his face. But he was all cop now. He had his gaze pin-pointed on Ian. She wanted Bo to shoot him or do whatever it took to stop this, but Bo couldn't do that because Ian had positioned her in front of him.

"Stop right where you are," Ian said when Bo took another step closer. "If you move, Mattie dies. If she moves, you die. Your choice."

Some choice. Mattie didn't intend to let that happen.

"Backup will be here soon," Bo informed him. "They'll do a silent approach, no sirens.

So you won't even know they're here until they're already in position. Let's end this now before they arrive."

Ian laughed. "I can only imagine what your idea of ending it is. I'm sure you've already gotten into Arturo's safety deposit box so you know what's going on."

But they didn't know, because they hadn't gotten into the box yet. What was Ian talking about?

Mattie tried a different approach. "What do you want from me?"

Because Ian's chest was right against her back, she felt him stiffen. "I want what I've always wanted—you. I love you, Mattie. I always have."

Oh, yes. He was crazy. But knowing that didn't help the situation. Insane people couldn't be reasoned with, and God knows how Ian was planning to show her how much he'd always loved her.

"Before supercop here got in the way, I was just going to take you with me," Ian added. He was angry now and pressed the gun harder into her temple. "No one would have gotten hurt, and it wouldn't have come down to this."

"This?" she repeated. "You're trying to kidnap me."

"No. I knew if we spent some time alone, you'd see that I was the man you really loved. Not Brody. And definitely not this cop."

"Listen to what you're saying," Bo challenged. "You say you love her, but you're ready to kill her. That doesn't make sense."

"Yes, it does." His voice was different now. An eerie calmness replaced the anger. "Because if I can't have her, no one can. Mattie's always been mine."

Bo took a step closer, and from the corner of her eye Mattie saw the dark green car approach. Backup, no doubt. She didn't doubt the cops would try to get themselves into a position to end this, but Ian still had the gun pointed to her head. And since he was crazy, he could kill her and then try to end his own life.

Maybe Bo would live, and that would mean Jacob and Holly would have at least one parent.

She felt Ian move a little, and she glanced back. He'd seen the dark green car. He knew there wasn't much time before this would escalate or he would have to surrender.

Mattie feared surrender was the last thing on Ian's mind.

"Let her go," Bo ordered again. "Right now, you'd just be charged with kidnapping. You're a lawyer. You know you can pull an insanity plea. You can walk away from this and just get time in a mental facility."

Even though she hated the thought of Ian being out in just a few years, that was better than any alternative she could come up with.

"True. I could do that," Ian conceded. "If it weren't for that damn safety deposit box. I swear I didn't know Arturo was smart enough to cover his butt that way. Too bad. Because his attempt to protect himself means my plan is all screwed up. I can't pin any of this on Kendall or Tolivar. I have nothing to lose."

She looked at Bo, who shook his head. Obviously, he didn't know anything about this, either. But it sounded as if that safety deposit box contained some kind of information that would incriminate Ian.

"Ian, what did you do?" Mattie demanded.

"What didn't I do?" Ian countered.

Ian had the seat already pushed all the way back, and he began to maneuver her deeper inside the car. He also tipped the gun away from her head.

And he aimed it at Bo.

"And it was all for you," Ian whispered to her. "Before this is over, you might appreciate that. You might learn to love me the way I love you."

"Never."

It might not be wise to make him angrier than he already was, but Mattie figured she had to do something. Ian was trying to get them into a position so he could drive away with her. And shoot Bo. If she could just get Ian to move the gun, just a little more to the right, then she could ram him with her elbow again and not risk him getting a shot off in Bo's direction.

"Never is a long time," Ian growled. He gave her another adjustment. She was still in his lap, but now she was behind the wheel. Mattie glanced down and saw the keys already in the ignition. "I can change your mind. Where I'm taking you, all we'll have is time."

That made her skin crawl.

"First, though," Ian added, "I have just one tiny piece of unfinished business."

He meant Bo. Ian was going to try to kill him, and Bo wouldn't be able to return fire, because despite the new position, she was still in the way.

What she was about to say was risky, but anything at this point was risky. "I could never love you, Ian. I'm in love with Bo."

Since her attention was fastened to Bo, she

saw him blink, and he was no doubt asking himself if she meant it.

She did.

It was the worst possible timing, but Mattie realized it was the truth. She was in love with Bo.

"You're in love with him?" Ian snapped. He put the gun back to her head. "You're lying."

"No. I'm not." And the truth was there, right in her voice. She could hear it. Bo could, as well.

And obviously so did Ian.

Ian yelled, a feral sound that pierced through her right ear, and she felt his arm tense.

He was about to pull the trigger.

Mattie drew back her elbow and rammed it into his belly as hard as she could. But it was too late.

The shot blasted through the car.

THE BLOOD RUSHED to Bo's head when he saw what was about to happen. He shouted for Mattie to get down, but the sound of his voice was drowned out by the bullet that Ian fired.

A thousand things went through Bo's mind, none good. He had been a cop long enough to know that a point-blank shot was usually fatal.

He raced to the car, to the tangle of bodies, and he was terrified of what he might see there. In that moment, that one horrible moment, Bo was aware of just how much Mattie meant to him.

He couldn't lose her. It couldn't be too late to save her.

Bo shifted his angle to the side, and he saw her moving inside the car. Thank God. She was alive. That didn't mean she wasn't hurt, though. It was the same for Ian. There was still a fight going on between Mattie and him, and Ian still had his gun.

Bo wanted to reach inside and try to pull Mattie out, but he couldn't take the chance. He couldn't tell if Mattie was somehow restraining Ian's shooting hand. If he wrenched her from the vehicle, that might give Ian the perfect opportunity to fire another shot.

And this one might be fatal.

Bo was aware that backup had arrived. From the corner of his eye, he saw them making their way toward him. They had their guns drawn, ready to help, but no one could help right now. He watched the struggle, trying to figure out how to get Mattie out of there alive.

She twisted her body, her head whiplashing against the seat. Ian had shoved her, and in that shove, he had created just enough space for Bo to see that Mattie had a death grip on Ian's right wrist. That prevented Ian from shooting directly at Mattie, but that meant he could use his left hand to punch her. And that's what the man was doing.

Ian landed a punch right to Mattie's face.

No amount of willpower and training would have stopped Bo at that point. He couldn't stand by and watch Ian beat her to a pulp.

Bo holstered his own gun so he could use his hands, and so Ian couldn't use it against him if this fight got worse than it already was. Bo was ready for *worse*. He was ready to kill this guy with his bare hands.

It was a tight fit, but Bo managed to reach into the car. Ian must have seen him coming because he started to fight harder, and he rammed his fist into Mattie's jaw again. Somehow, she held on to to his wrist.

And Bo helped.

He latched on to the gun itself. He couldn't wrench it from Ian's hand, but it freed up Mattie to move back.

"Get out of here!" Bo told her.

Bo cursed when Ian got in another punch, this one landing on the side of Mattie's head.

She cursed, too, and fought to get away. Because they were all crammed into the small space between the seat, the console and the steering wheel, there wasn't much room to maneuver.

Ian turned his head and sank his teeth into Bo's hand. The pain shot through him, but Bo didn't let go because that was the hand he was using to try to control the gun.

"You sick piece of slime!" Mattie yelled at Ian. She caught hold of Ian's hair and rammed his head against the console.

That stopped the biting, but Ian came after Mattie again. Before the man could punch her again, Bo caught Mattie's arm and slung her out of the way. She landed behind him somewhere, and that meant he could grab Ian with both hands.

Bo dragged him from the car.

"I'll kill her!" Ian shouted. And he kept shouting it while he tried to bash his gun against Bo's head.

Bo's anger level was beyond dangerous, and that last attempt to kill Mattie pushed him over the edge. Bo slammed Ian face first against the car.

Ian gasped and wheezed for breath, and Bo couldn't believe it when the SOB tried to aim the gun.

At Mattie.

Ian was going to try to shoot her.

"Get down," Bo told Mattie.

Just as Ian pulled the trigger.

Bo didn't look back to see where the shot had landed, but he prayed Mattie had gotten out of the way in time. He put all his anger and attention on Ian. Bo rammed his full weight against Ian's back, and he bashed the man's right hand against the car. When Ian still held on, Bo whacked his hand again.

And again.

The gun finally dislodged and went crashing onto the ground. Ian gave up, too, and sagged against the car.

"Mattie, are you all right?" Bo asked, and he held his breath.

"I'm okay."

Well, she sure as hell didn't sound okay, so he glanced at her. Mattie didn't look okay, either. Her mouth was bleeding, and she had a cut on her cheekbone. God knows how many bruises she had on her. She was pale and shaking, but she hadn't been shot. Bo thanked God for that, because Ian had had several chances to shoot her.

Bo tipped his head, and the other officers moved in. He waited, holding Ian in place, until one of the officers kicked Ian's gun out of the way, and the other officer came in to cuff the man and read him his rights.

Bo watched, hoping like hell that Ian would try something. He wanted the moron to come at him again so he could pulverize him.

"Don't," Mattie whispered. She touched Bo's arm and rubbed gently. "Let it go."

"Can you?" Bo snapped. The emotion was still raw and angry and roaring through him.

"Yes. Because Ian doesn't matter. He'll go to jail for the rest of his life. You and I, on the other hand, are free. No more danger. We can spend the rest of our lives with Jacob and Holly."

With just those words and her touch, she soothed him and lessened his anger over Ian's attack. She reminded Bo of what was really at stake here.

Ian cursed, apparently upset that Mattie could find a silver lining so soon after the hell she'd just been through.

Ian stopped cursing, and much to Bo's surprise, he laughed. "Don't go planning any happily-ever-afters, Mattie," he spat out. "Because once you listen to what's in that safety deposit box, you're not going to be able to live with yourself."

Chapter Nineteen

Mattie stared at the safety deposit box that Captain Tolbert placed on the center of the table in the crime lab. She hadn't expected the police to bring the entire box so it could be analyzed, but here it was.

Like a rattlesnake coiled and ready to strike.

"Ian was probably lying about what's inside there," Bo assured her.

He slipped his arm around her and pressed a kiss to her forehead, just above the bandage. The stitches she'd gotten just a half hour earlier were starting to sting now, and she felt achy and bruised from the fight with Ian. Yet, those were minor things. Bo and she were alive, the children were safe, and Ian wouldn't be able to hurt them anymore. The only thing left to deal with was the box and what might be inside. Oh, and of course, there was Bo.

She needed to deal with him, too.

"We got the court order," the captain explained. "So, it's open. I first had it tested to make sure there were no explosives or booby traps. There weren't. So I had a look inside while you two were with the medics."

Mattie's gaze whipped to the captain's so she could see if there were any hints of what she was about to face. He was somber. His expression seemed to say, "I'm sorry."

She took a deep breath, leaned over the stainless steel table and opened it. There were papers, a small tape recorder and a gun.

"What is all of this?" Bo asked, tightening his grip on her.

"Terrance Arturo obviously didn't trust Kaplan, even though he was working for him." The captain took out the first piece of paper and handed it to Mattie. "He explains that Kaplan hired him to break into the Witness Protection files so he could find you. There are numbers for the offshore account where Kaplan deposited the money, and Arturo even tells us how to trace the money back to Kaplan."

Well, that certainly wasn't bad news. "And the gun?"

"According to Arturo, it was the weapon he used to kill your fiancé. We'll run ballistics, but we're pretty sure it'll be a match."

He paused. "Arturo says Kaplan's prints are on the gun because he's the one who gave it to Arturo."

So it was yet more proof that would keep Ian in jail for life or maybe even get him the death penalty.

"I've gone through the papers," the captain continued, "and from what I can tell, Kaplan set up Collier in that illegal arms deal. Your uncle did try to cover it up afterward, so he's not completely innocent, but all the attempts to kidnap and kill you came from Kaplan."

"Kendall's innocent?" Bo asked, sounding as surprised as she was.

"Almost. He threatened Mattie so she wouldn't testify against him, and that's why she was placed in Witness Protection, but there's no proof that he would have actually killed her. The real threat was Kaplan all along. I think Kaplan set things up to make it look as if Collier wanted her dead."

"But you said Collier tried to cover up the arms deal," Bo pointed out.

"Yes, and he might have to face charges for that. But we might be able to cut him a deal if he'll testify against Kaplan."

Which he would be a fool not to do. Kendall might be ruthless in business, but he wasn't stupid.

"What about Marshal Tolivar?" Bo asked.

"Innocent, too. There's proof in these papers that Kaplan set him up, as well."

Mattie shook her head. How could one man have tried to ruin so many lives? Worse, he'd nearly succeeded.

Mattie glanced at the last item in the box. "What's on the tape recorder?" she asked the captain.

The captain paused as though unsure how to give her the bad news.

"I'll listen to it," Bo volunteered. "I can summarize what's on it." He kissed her forehead again. "Rosalie will be here with the kids any minute and you can spend time with them in my office."

It was a generous offer. She did want to spend time with Jacob and Holly. And Bo. But she had to know what was on that tape.

Mattie stared at the captain. "Ian said I wouldn't be able to live with myself after I listen to what's in the box."

The captain mumbled some profanity. "He is obviously a psychopath. He created a vile situation, and when it didn't work out the way he wanted, he blamed you. You have nothing to feel guilty about, Mattie."

"What's on the tape?" she insisted.

The captain glanced at Bo first. "It's a

recording of Kaplan meeting with your fiancé, Brody. Arturo's in the room."

"Arturo recorded it?" Bo asked.

Captain Tolbert nodded. "Kaplan offers Brody a deal—leave Mattie, move out of the country, and Kaplan will let him live. Brody tells Kaplan that he won't leave, that he won't hurt Mattie that way. That's when Kaplan orders Arturo to kill him."

Even though Mattie hadn't been there, she could almost see it. Ian had probably thought Brody would jump at the chance to live, but he had chosen her instead.

And Brody had died because of it.

Bo cursed under his breath. "Don't you dare let Ian get to you like this." Bo no doubt saw the tears in her eyes. "Ian and Arturo killed Brody. Not you. This isn't on you."

As if to convince her of that, Bo kissed her. It wasn't a peck of reassurance like the others. This was a real kiss. It shouldn't have made any difference in what she was feeling.

But it did.

Bo pulled back and lifted her chin to meet her eye-to-eye. "If Ian had offered you the same deal today, to give up the person you love or die, would you take it?"

Mattie didn't even have to think about this. "No."

"Neither would I. Because love is worth fighting for. And yes, sometimes it's worth dying for."

"Like today," she whispered. She had certainly been willing to die to stop Ian from killing Bo.

"Brody didn't have a chance to fight for his life. Ian took that away from him. But don't let Ian take away anything else. Don't let him stop you from reaching out and taking what's right in front of you."

The tears returned to her eyes, because Bo was right. The person she loved more than life itself was standing right in front of her.

And that person was Bo.

"The past is the past," Bo said, as if still trying to convince her. "Yes, part of you will always love Brody. Part of me will always love Nadine. But this is now, Mattie. This is the present and the future, and I want to spend that present and future with you."

The captain cleared his throat, reminding them that he was still in the room. She'd forgotten all about him, mainly because the only thing she could see and feel right now was Bo. He'd said just the right thing to put things into perspective. She couldn't let a deranged man like Ian ruin her chance at happiness by trying to weigh her down with old baggage. Baggage Ian had created.

"Maybe I should just step out for a couple of minutes," the captain mumbled.

Neither of them stopped him.

"You told Ian you were in love with me," Bo continued. "Is it true?" But he didn't wait for her to answer. "I need it to be true."

Mattie came up on her toes and kissed him. "It's true."

He smiled against her mouth. "Good. Because I'm in love with you, too."

Everything inside her turned to warm silk. How could anything feel this right, this perfect? She had only known Bo a few days, but she knew she wanted to spend the rest of her life with him. She was about to tell him that, too, but he kissed her again, and her world tipped on its axis.

He pressed her against the stainless table, in the sterile, cold room that was suddenly warm and welcoming.

Bo must have heard the sound at the same moment she did because he pulled away from her and went to the door through which the captain had just exited. But it wasn't the captain returning. Mattie recognized that sound.

It was Holly, and she was giggling.

Mattie hurried to the door and saw Rosalie making her way down the hall toward them. Jacob was toddling across the glossy tiles, and since he looked ready to fall, Rosalie had a hand on him. In the crook of her other arm was Holly, who was apparently laughing at her brother's antics.

"Hope we're not interrupting," Rosalie said. She leaned down and placed Holly on the floor, as well. "But they were ready to take your office apart. Figured they'd do less damage down here."

"You're not interrupting," Bo volunteered. "I was just about to ask Mattie to marry me, but it's probably better if I do it in front of all of you, anyway."

Mattie felt her mouth drop open. But she also felt the love race through her. The moment had already been perfect, but Bo had found a way to make it even better.

Bo reached down and picked up Holly when she made her way toward him, and he kissed her on her cheek. He passed her to Mattie so she could do the same. The little girl smiled, pressed both of her chubby hands to the sides of Mattie's face and gave her a big kiss.

"Ma," Holly announced.

Obviously not wanting to be left out of the action, Jacob strung together several Ma Mas, and he tugged at Mattie's dress. Mattie bent down and scooped him up, as well.

Rosalie smiled and blinked back tears. "Well? Seems you owe Bo an answer about that marriage proposal."

"My answer is yes," Mattie whispered. Just for Bo. But then she repeated it, louder, so the children and Rosalie would hear.

Rosalie clapped and wiped the tears from her face.

Jacob picked up on the clapping and did the same. Holly soon joined him for the celebration. Even though they were too young to know what her yes meant, they obviously knew this was a happy time for their new family.

Mattie's arms were already full, but she managed to turn to Bo so she could kiss him the way she wanted. A kiss to let him know that their future would always be filled with love. Like now. Forever.

* * * * *

LARGER-PRINT BOOKS!

GET 2 FREE LARGER-PRINT NOVELS

PLUS 2 FREE GIFTS!

HARLEQUIN®
INTRIGUE®

Breathtaking Romantic Suspense

HILP10R